THE HONKY TONK BIG HOSS BOOGIE

A Nashville P.I. Series

ROBERT J. RANDISI

WOLFPACK
PUBLISHING
— EST 2013 —

BOOKS BY ROBERT J. RANDISI

Published in the United States by Wolfpack Publishing, Las Vegas.

Wolfpack Publishing
6032 Wheat Penny Avenue
Las Vegas, NV 89122

wolfpackpublishing.com

Paperback ISBN 978-1-64119-807-3
Ebook ISBN 978-1-64119-806-6

Library of Congress Control Number: 2019933151

THE HONKY TONK BIG HOSS BOOGIE

PROLOGUE

The Present . . .

CORKY BARNES TOLD everyone who would listen that he was a "Major Country Music Producer." It wasn't a lie. He was, and he liked everybody to know it as soon as possible.

He stood at the window of his office, looking down at Music Row—his domain, or so he thought. Starcade Records was located right smack in the center of the Row. At night, from another part of the building, he could see the lights from downtown, even hear music from some of the clubs. The Wildhorse Saloon was only a mile or so away. Many of his artists had performed there over the years. Hell, most of the big names had played the Wild-horse at one time or another.

Last year, in May, the Cumberland had tried to swallow up Nashville. Music Row—a mile from the river—had been safe, but the downtown district, on the other side of I-65, the home of most of the clubs in town—Printers

Alley, 2nd Avenue, Lower Broadway—had been under water. That included the Wildhorse. And the Grand Ole Opry had five feet of water in their basement. There was millions in damage, but Nashville was coming back. Hell, even an Act of God couldn't stop the music! Nashville was indestructible!

"Corky," Walter Rutlidge said, "we have to deal with this."

Barnes turned from the window and looked at his long-time attorney and friend. They had graduated from college together. Barnes had gone into the music industry, and Rutlidge had gone to law school. Thirty years later they were still working together. Well, actually Walter Rutlidge the attorney worked for Starcade Records and the Major Country Music Producer. Outside of work, Walter and Corky were still friends, even though Corky thought Walter was kind of an asshole. He had no idea that the feeling was very mutual.

"Goldangit, Walt," Corky said, picking a huge cigar up from an ashtray on his desk and gesturing with it, "don't you think I know that, boy?"

"So what do you intend to do?"

Barnes walked to his desk, tapped it with his right forefinger while he thought.

"We need somebody," he said, finally. "Somebody we can trust to do whatever we tell 'em to do, you hear?"

"Andy Pac?"

"Hell no," Barnes said, "there's no dang point in involvin' the head of A&R in this. Or anyone else in the company, for that matter."

"Then . . . it would have to be somebody we paid," Rutlidge said. "Somebody who would do what we tell them because we're paying them. A lot."

"Get me somebody."

"Me?"

"You're the lawyer," Barnes said. "Don't you know some private eyes?"

"Yeah, I guess—"

"Mind you, I don't want some sleazy joker in a trench coat, though," Barnes said, sitting behind his desk. "I want a reliable, normal guy. I have to deal with enough assholes and weirdoes in this business."

Rutlidge didn't bother pointing out that Barnes was lucky he was dealing with Country artists and not Rock 'n Rollers. Now *those* people were weird.

Barnes settled back in his chair, stuck the cigar in his mouth, folded his hands and placed them on his protruding belly.

"So?"

Walter Rutlidge had a very thoughtful look on his face. Barnes knew the look. When he made that expression, the lawyer usually had an idea. Not always good, but an idea.

"I may have somebody . . ."

"Who?"

"Augusto Velez-Colon."

"Who?"

"Auggie Velez. Do you know him?"

"No, I never heard of him. Who the blazes is he?"

"He's a session musician."

"Well, that's why I don't know him. I deal with the artists, the stars, not the dang back-up singers."

Rutlidge realized how true that was. The people who worked in the studios along Music Row knew Auggie Colon as a reliable session man and back-up singer. But Walter Rutlidge happened to know that Auggie also had a private investigator's license. He wasn't Jim Rockford or

Mike Hammer, though. He mostly served papers, took some photos, maybe a few tail jobs and pickups to supplement his income as a musician. All that experience made him a perfect choice to do what they needed to be done.

"So who is he?"

"The guy we need," Rutlidge explained why.

"What're we gonna have to pay him?" Barnes asked. "I don't wanna pay him a lot."

"Maybe not a lot, at all," Rutlidge said. "We might be able to trade for something else."

"Like what?"

"Well, Auggie's a musician," Rutlidge said. "Came to Nashville about eight years ago. He's managed to make a good name for himself as reliable, but there's something else he wants. Something they all want when they come here."

"A recordin' deal of his own."

"Right."

Barnes shook his head. "These folks got no imagination. How old is he?"

"Mid-thirties, I guess."

"Not a golden' chance," Barnes said. "Too old. When it comes to handin' out recordin' deals, we need another Scotty McCreary, not some old guy in his thirties."

"Old guy? He's almost twenty years younger than we are, Corky."

"Yeah, but for a lawyer and a Major Country Music Producer, we're in our dang prime."

"I get it."

"So, do you know this here fella?"

"I've used him to serve some papers a time or two. I can call him."

"Good." He removed the cigar from his mouth and

pointed it at Rutlidge. "Do it. Offer him the goin' rate for a sleazy private eye, and a possible recordin' deal."

"I'll get him to come and see you," Rutlidge said, "but you're going to make the offers."

"Fine," Barnes said, "fine, whatever. But Walter . . ." he wagged a thick forefinger at his friend, "this stays between us, boy. I mean, he don't have to know everythin', you hear?"

"Don't worry, Boss," Rutlidge said, "there's no reason he has to know much of *any*thing."

PART 1

"I don't say cain't,
I don't say ain't,
an' I don't say Momma,
but that don't mean I'm not country."

Augusto Velez-Colon

1

Three weeks later . . .

I GOT off the bus with a backpack and a guitar case. The scratchy, burning feeling behind my eyes reminded me of why I do session work and don't go on the road much, anymore.

A friend of mine who played with Gretchen Wilson's band called me and said they had an emergency. They were in the middle of their tour and needed someone to play rhythm guitar. The regular guy had an accident, fell off the stage and broke his wrist. He'd told Gretchen he knew somebody who might be available at a moment's notice. That was me. Usually at home, in Nashville, I did primarily session work. Coincidentally, I didn't have anything scheduled for a few weeks, and—as always—I could use the money. In my other business, I was a private investigator, but I didn't have any work in that area, either.

I was able to travel light, bringing only my own Fender

acoustic. The regular guy was still with the tour along with his six guitars, which I was able to use. He hung around, working with the roadies because—God only knew why—he enjoyed being there.

But now I was back. It was eight A.M., and I wanted nothing more than to be in my own bed. I walked the few blocks to my place—a loft in Printers Alley, above the Bourbon Street Blues and Boogie Bar. I had done a favor for the owners a few years back. As a result, they offered to rent me the upstairs for a fraction of what they could have gotten. I only accepted because I needed a place, intending to move when I found something better, within a few weeks—months, at the most. I was still looking . . .

I turned down my block, which two years ago had been under three feet of water from the overflowing Cumberland River. Nashville had been waterlogged for months, but the music never stopped—it just moved. The clubs were back now, on 2nd Street and Broadway, with some of the best right on my block, like the Boogie, the Fiddle, and Steel and, if you were partial to open mike night, Lonnie's Western.

I trudged up the stairs, ready to flop into bed without even taking off my boots. I unlocked the door, stepped inside, picked up the mail scattered on the floor. I locked the door behind me, set down my backpack and guitar case, then went to find something in the frig to drink that hadn't gone bad while I was gone.

I found some orange juice and drank it down. That would have to do until I got some sleep.

I flipped a couple of wall switches, and my 1800-foot loft lit up, welcoming me home. It was all one room under a high ceiling; windows ran almost from floor to ceiling and overlooked Printers Alley. There was a kitchen area with a refrigerator, coffee maker and microwave, a small kitchen table: no stove, no oven. I made do with fresh fruit and used the microwave to warm food I brought home with me. And at the far end, a king-sized bed. Most of the rest of the area was taken up by a home studio: recording equipment, a piano, half a dozen guitars, music stands, microphones. It was far from a professionally equipped studio, but it was the best I could afford to put together. I wrote songs there, practiced, invited other musicians up to jam, and sometimes recorded what we played.

At the moment, though, I'd had enough of music for a while. My ears were still ringing from two weeks of performing with Gretchen and her band. Touring always meant electric guitars, powerful amps, screaming fans, and partial deafness for a few days after it was all over. Which was why I preferred acoustic guitars.

I took the bandana off my head and scratched my shaved dome. I wasn't vain, the bandana just looked better, especially on stage. I was on my way to the bed when I heard a pounding on my door. Suddenly, the bed was further away. I thought about ignoring the sound, but it soon became obvious whoever was there wasn't going away.

I turned, went to the door and opened it.

"What the—" I said, but was cut off as two guys stormed into the room.

"Augusto Velez-Colon?" one of them asked.

"That's my name, dude, but I go by Auggie Velez." I had been named for my grandfather, Augusto Velez who—when he came to this country from Puerto Rico—added his wife's maiden name "Colon" to the end of his name because there were so many Velez's already in the U.S.

"Mr. Velez," one of them said, "my name's Detective Hollinger, this is my partner, Detective Lewis. We're with Nashville P.D., Homicide Division." They showed me their badges. "We need you to come with us."

"Homicide?" I said. "Boys, that's way out of my league. I'm a musician—"

"With a PI's ticket, right?" Lewis asked.

"Well, yeah, but—"

"Mr. Velez," Hollinger said, "we need to discuss this downtown."

"Detective Hollinger, we can't get much more downtown than this."

I actually wasn't sure if their offices at James Robertson Parkway were further downtown than Printers Alley was. It might have been a tie. Either way, we could have each spit and hit the Cumberland.

Hollinger looked around, took in my home. He had a boyish look to him, with red hair and freckles, but I believed him to be my age. His partner was fifty or so, starting to spread out in the middle. He chewed gum that filled the air with the smell of pineapple.

"That's a lot of guitars," he said. "You collect?"

"One or two of them are collectible," I said, "but mostly I play them."

"Mr. Velez, we've been looking for you for a couple of weeks," Lewis said.

"I've been on tour. Just got back a few minutes ago."

"We know, we've been watching the place," Hollinger said.

"You want me that bad?" I asked. "What's it all about that it can't wait for me to get a few hours of shuteye?"

"As we said," Hollinger answered, "we've been waiting two weeks."

"And a few hours will make that much difference?" I asked.

"Mr. Velez," Detective Hollinger said, "we're gonna have to insist."

"Don't make us get insistent," Lewis said.

I looked at each of them in turn, then said, "You dudes have a good act."

Lewis took hold of my arm. The guy had a vice grip, and as tired as I was, I knew I'd never break it.

"I guess I'm comin'," I said, picking up my bandana.

2

It was a one-minute, quarter-of-a-mile drive from Printers Alley to 200 James Robertson Parkway. The only thing I learned for sure during that minute was that their offices were closer to the river than my loft was.

I had never been inside the Nashville P.D. building before. Even when I did have some PI work to do, legal papers to serve, evidence to deliver, I sort of circled it— the Davidson County Court House, Sheriff's Department, etc.

They walked me through the building to an interview room and sat me inside at a table.

"We'll be right back," Lewis said.

"Do you want anything? Some coffee?" Hollinger asked.

"Yeah, that'd be good. Black."

Hollinger nodded and they both left. I looked around, didn't see a mirror, so they weren't watching me. I suppose they wanted to leave me alone to think for a while but think about what? I had no idea what this was all about. Before I'd left to do two weeks on tour, I hadn't been involved in anything. My docket was clean—both musically, and legally—which was why I'd been able to pick up and leave and meet the band on the road.

I could have put my head down and slept, but I was afraid they'd think that meant I was guilty of something. They say a guilty man knows he belongs in jail, and so can sleep there. I fought to keep my eyes open.

They came back almost an hour later, carrying several containers of coffee. Hollinger set one down on the table and pushed it over to me, then put down a file folder. He pulled a chair out and sat. Lewis remained standing, leaned against the wall and drank his coffee. I took the plastic top off mine and sipped it. It was warm, not hot. They'd bought it and let it stand a while.

"Thanks," I said.

"Time to tell us a story, Auggie. You mind if I call you Auggie?"

"I don't mind," I said, "and what story do you want to hear?"

"The story about you, and a man named Nolan, Felix Nolan."

"I don't know a guy named Felix Nolan," I said. "Pick someone else. You wanna hear about me and Gretchen Wilson?"

That woke Lewis up. He pushed away from the wall and stood up straight.

"What's that about Gretchen Wilson?"

"That's who I've been on tour with the past two weeks."

"And what about you and her?" the older detective asked.

"Nothin'," I said. "She's a sweet kid."

"Then why'd you say—"

"I was just jokin'," I said.

"Dave," Hollinger said, "relax. He was just kidding. Why don't you go get some more coffee?"

Lewis gave me a dirty look and left the room.

"He's a big Gretchen Wilson fan," Hollinger said.

"He doesn't have much of a sense of humor, does he?" I asked.

"No," Hollinger said. "He's kind of serious about everything—especially country music. He loves it."

"I go more for country blues, myself," I said.

"But you just said you were on tour—"

"I take jobs when I need money, Detective," I said. "I've done session work on lots of country albums, even some rock."

"We're getting off the subject," he said.

"What was the subject again?" I asked.

"Felix Nolan."

"Don't know him."

"Well, we have information that indicates you do."

"Look," I said, "the name doesn't ring a bell, but if you tell me what's going on maybe I can come up with something helpful, anyway."

He stared at me for a few moments.

"Okay," he said, finally. He opened the folder, took out a photo and set it down in front of me. "That's Felix Nolan."

My mouth went dry. The guy in the photo was obviously dead. Looking at dead people isn't my scene. I pushed it back at him.

"Don't tell me a big, bad private eye like you is squeamish," he said.

"I don't usually deal with murder."

"Aren't you partners with Harley Rayhorn?"

"I am. So?"

"He's been around a long time, probably knows where all the bodies are buried."

"That's Harley's business, not mine."

"He's kind of washed up, isn't he?"

"He's doing okay," I said. "He took me on to do a lot of the legwork, some computer work."

"Trying to move with the times, huh?" Hollinger said. "Most of the old-timers have hung it up."

"Harley's the best in the business."

"Maybe he was, at one time, but . . ."

I took a sip of my coffee. I wasn't only feeling sick because of the picture but because—even though I didn't recognize the guy why else would they be showing me a picture of him unless . . .

"You must not be much of a poker player, Auggie," Hollinger said. "It's all over your face that you know this guy."

"I don't know him," I said, "but I'm not stupid. What do you know?"

"We know you met with him. He had your name in his pocket, and the name of Corky Barnes, from Starcade Records. You want to tell me what you and Starcade have in common?"

"It was about three weeks before I left to go on tour . . ."

3

Three weeks ago . . .

I WAS FOOLING around on my new mandolin when my phone rang. I was thinking that maybe learning the new instrument might get me additional session work, and also help inspire some new songs. I was doing okay lately with lyrics, but when it came to the melody, I was running dry.

Sometimes I just let the machine pick up, other times I'll turn it off and let the phone ring. And if I'm deep into a song and I'm recording, I turn the ringer off. On that day, however, I decided to take a break and answer the dang thing.

I walked to the phone with my Little Martin hanging from my neck. I'd been walking around the loft, trying to work out some riffs. I spend a lot of time with a guitar hanging from my neck, even when I'm not working.

"Hello?"

"Auggie?"

"Yo."

"Walter Rutlidge here."

I knew Rutlidge. He was an attorney I used to do some process serving for before Harley took me on as a partner. He was also an asshole. He worked for Corky Barnes at Starcade Records, was always promising me an introduction, but never came through.

"I'm not available, Walter," I said, even though I was.

"I don't need you to serve any papers, Auggie," Rutlidge said. "It's something else, entirely."

"Like what?"

"Do you still want to meet Corky Barnes?"

"Oh no," I said, "you're not gonna get me with that again. You've made too many promises to introduce me—"

"No, no, Auggie," Rutlidge said. "This is legit. Corky needs a PI to do something for him, and I recommended you."

Immediately, I was suspicious. Rutlidge was not my friend or benefactor. Why would he recommend me?

"Why me, Walter?"

"Because he said he didn't want anyone sleazy," Rutlidge said, "and he wanted somebody he could trust."

Well, I wasn't sleazy and, even though I'd never been a boy scout, I did consider myself trustworthy, but this still sounded hinky to me.

"Walter, I'm still wondering why—"

"Auggie, this is a paying job," Rutlidge said. "Don't you still need paying jobs?"

"Well, yeah, sure—"

"And it's a chance to meet Corky," he went on. "You still want to meet Corky, don't you?"

"Yeah—"

"Look, be at the Starcade offices today at two P.M.,"

Rutlidge said. "Corky will be waiting for you. And if you don't show up—"

"I have a session this morning, Walter," I said, checking my watch. "In fact, if I don't leave now I'll be late. It's down the street from you, so I should be able to make it by three."

"Okay, fine," he said. "Three's okay—but be here, Auggie."

"I'll be there, Walter," I said. Even if it was just to satisfy my curiosity. "I'll be there."

THE STARCADE RECORDS Building was located right in the center of Music Row, on the corner of Music Square East and Chet Atkins Place (Roy Acuff also had a street named after him). The Row is just on the other side of I-65, a long walk from my place. I decided to take the bus, which let me off on Demonbreun near 16th Street. Where Demonbreun and Division Streets come together with Music Square East and 16th Avenue South is the Music Row Roundabout, which is supposed to assure a good flow of traffic through the area. Adjacent to that is Owen Bradley Park. Bradley was a famous songwriter, performer, and later, a publisher.

I walked into the park, wearing my Slash T-shirt this time (and his Les Paul Signature guitar), and a blue bandana to match the blue hand-tooling on my Rocketbuster boots. I figured I'd see Jasmine near the life-sized statue of Bradley seated behind a piano. She usually spent a few hours, several days a week, at this location, playing her guitar for the public. She wasn't begging for money, but her guitar case was open, and if anyone saw fit to drop a bill or two in there, that was okay with her.

Spotting her, I stopped to watch for a few moments. She was playing and singing one of her original songs. She was blond and plain- looking, could have been anywhere from thirty to fifty, wearing a fringed skirt and cowgirl shirt. She was a staple in the park, performing her very odd songs for mostly no audience. Jasmine's music was an acquired taste. From the looks on the faces of the people passing by—and her empty guitar case—no one had acquired it, yet.

Starcade was a few blocks from the park. Between them was the recording studio I was due at. I had agreed to do a two-hour session with some musicians I knew, laying down some tracks that would later be incorporated into some Blake Shelton recordings. I was doing it because I liked Blake, had played live with him a few times and considered us almost friends. (No, I wasn't invited to the wedding.)

As I entered, the girl at the front desk looked up and smiled. Her name was Linda, and whenever I did any work there, we flirted but had never seen each other without that desk between us.

"Hey, Good-lookin'," she said. "What brings you here?"

"Booked for two hours to lay down some tracks. Is Elton Mott here?"

"Oh, the Blake Shelton session? Yes, he's in number four."

"Thanks, Linda."

I went through a door, walked down a corridor and entered studio 4. Nick Chandler, the engineer, was sitting at the mixing desk, which was lit up like a Christmas tree. There also a twenty-seven-inch computer screen in front of him. He swiveled around in his chair, spread his arms, gave me a big smile, then leaned into the mike, keyed it and said, "He's here!"

Sitting in the corner was a girl who looked about 18 or 19, wearing a top that was so skimpy even her small breasts seemed about to spill out. She smiled at me and I could see she wore braces on her upper teeth. I assumed she was a friend of Nick's. He was in his 30's but had a liking for young girls who impressed easily.

"Am I last?" I asked.

"As long as you're here," Nick said, extending his hand. I switched my guitar case to my left and shook with my right. "Good to see you, Auggie."

"You, too, Nick."

I entered the studio and got some mock applause from Elton and his guys.

"Thought you were gonna be late," he said. "You know the guys? Guys, Auggie Velez."

I knew the drummer, Andy Kane. We'd played together before. He and Elton were my age. I knew the other two younger guys by sight, though we hadn't worked together. I shook hands all around, then opened my case and took out my Fender acoustic. Elton had told me not to worry about anything electric; he'd supply those.

He came in close and asked, "What's goin' on, dude? You just made it. Time is money, you know?"

"I got a call just as I was leaving," I said.

"Important?"

"I've got an appointment with Corky Barnes at Starcade."

"Holy cow!" he said. "Get out! That's awesome, dude!"

"Don't get so excited," I said. "He wants to see me because of my other job."

"Corky Barnes needs a private eye and called you? Still awesome."

"His lawyer, Walter Rutlidge, called," I said. "I've done some work for him and he recommended me."

"At least that gets you in the front door."

I looked at my watch. "I told them I'd be there by three."

"Well, you should make it, unless somebody fucks up today. You gonna fuck up?"

"Not me."

"There ya go."

"Do you want to get something to eat after my meeting?"

"Well . . ." he said. I knew what he was thinking.

"On me," I said. "How about Noshville? About four?"

"Dude, you sure you'll be done by then?"

I shrugged. "Whatever we talk about, it should take no more than that for me to say yes or no."

"Okay," he said, "that sounds excellent. I've been craving a good bagel—among other things."

"Good," I said, "So let's get to work."

4

ELTON HAD SHEET MUSIC FOR ME, BUT I KNEW SOME OF the Blake Shelton stuff we were going to do, already. Blake was one of the nicest guys in the business and, if possible, had gotten even nicer since marrying Miranda Lambert. I was supposed to back him at the CMA's in about a month.

We did a quick run through and then got to work laying down the tracks. Elton was in charge, so when he waved his hands for us to stop we all stopped and listened to what he had to say. Nick never minded, he just sat at the board with his arms folded and waited, because he was getting paid by the hour.

Nobody fucked up and we got all the tracks down with some time to spare. I left the studio about ten-to-three, reaffirming that I'd meet Elton at Noshville at four. Shook hands all around, flirted some more with Linda, and left.

I walked a couple of blocks, passing studios I'd recorded in, smaller record label offices. Starcade, though, that was top of the line. Corky Barnes—by his own admission—was a starmaker. I didn't necessarily want to be a star, but I did want to get my own music out there, without footing the bill myself. That had been my dream when I first came to Nashville eight years ago. The dream had some tarnish on it these days, but it was still there. I just had to shine it every once in a while.

I took the elevator to the eighth floor, found the door with Barnes's name on it, followed by a lot of letters and titles—President, CEO, stuff like that—and entered.

I was greeted by a girl who looked like she could've been the recent winner of America's Next Top Model.

"Good afternoon," she said. "Can I help you?"

"Auggie Velez for Corky Barnes. I have a three o'clock."

"Yes, of course, Mr. Velez," she said. "I'll just tell him you're here."

She picked up the phone and announced me, then hung up and said, "Someone will be right out."

"Thanks." I spent about five minutes studying Gold and Platinum records that adorned the walls before Walter Rutledge appeared.

"Auggie," he said, extending his hand. "Glad you could make it." As usual, he was impeccable in a three-piece suit.

I shook his hand and asked, "Is Corky here?"

"Of course, of course," Rutledge said, slapping me on the back. "Come on; I'll take you back." He looked at the girl and said, "Thank you, Allegra."

"Of course, Mr. Rutledge," she said, without looking at him. I didn't have to be Magnum PI to realize she thought he was an asshole, too.

CORKY BARNES WAS SEATED behind a desk befitting a man who referred to himself as a "Major Country Music Producer." I'd heard him tell Crook & Chase that, also mention it in interviews I'd read in *Billboard* and several Nashville magazines. He was also a man of some girth and was an imposing figure as he sat behind his desk.

"Corky Barnes," Rutlidge said, as we entered, "meet Auggie Velez."

"My boy," Barnes said, standing up. He remained behind the desk but extended his hand. I had to step forward to shake it. Point for him.

"Mr. Barnes," I said. "It's a pleasure to meet you."

"You just call me Corky, boy," Barnes said. "Walter tells me you're a good man. Trustworthy."

"I like to think so," I said. "I'd also like to know why I'm here if you don't mind."

"Not at all," he said. "I admire me a fella who gets right to the point. Have a seat, son."

I knew that Rutlidge and Barnes had similar educations, but you couldn't tell that from the way they talked. Corky was a good ole boy Boss Hog type, talking real loud in a thick Southern accent and staring out at the world from beneath what I could only call a black 20-gallon hat. Rutlidge had no accent, at all. It's as if he trained to be a television announcer—a soft-spoken one.

He sat back down. I took the comfortable visitor's chair across from him. It was padded and had arms. From the corner of my eye, I could see Walter Rutlidge hovering on the side. There was a huge window behind Corky, but the rest of the walls in the room were covered with photos of him and the stars of Country Music. His desk was littered with Western paraphernalia he'd probably collected over the years—including a letter opener with a hand-tooled leather handle, a matching pencil and pen holder, the word "Cowboy" carved out of wood, and a small porcelain statue of Yosemite Sam. His western tastes even went to the string tie he was wearing. I made a silent bet with myself that he had cowboy boots tucked under his desk.

"Walter," Barnes said, "you're gonna make me dizzy. Light and set somewhere, boy."

"Sure, Corky."

Rutledge moved out of my view, sat down somewhere behind me. There was a sofa in the room, so I assumed he was there.

Corky was Walter's age, in his fifties. He'd been a name in Nashville for over twenty-five years, maybe longer. When I came to town eight years before, his was one of the first names I became aware of.

"Walter tells me you're a darn fine session musician," Corky said.

"I'm okay," I said.

"I think you're bein' a tad modest, boy."

"I understood I wasn't here as a musician," I said.

"No, that's true." Corky sat back, folded his hands over his belly, and looked past me. At that point, I became aware he was taking his cues from the lawyer. Something was up.

"To put what I need as plain as I can," Barnes said, "I need something delivered."

"What?"

Barnes held up his forefinger. "And I need it delivered without questions."

"Why? Oh, sorry. Delivered to who? And where? Sorry, again, but I'm afraid there does have to be some questions, Corky."

"If you agree to do this little ol' job for me," Barnes said, "you'll get all the info you need to make the delivery."

"Which means there will be things I won't know."

"You got it, son," he said. "What is it them government types say? Oh, yes, it's on a 'need to know' basis."

"Well," I said, folding my arms, "I think I'm going to have a problem with this."

He looked past me again, then said, "You ain't heard the deal, yet."

"Okay, what's the deal?"

"Five thousand."

"Dollars?"

"Yes."

What he didn't know was that I would have said "Dollars?" in that same tone of voice if he'd said a thousand.

"There are some questions I have to ask," I said. "How big is this . . . item I would need to deliver?"

"It fits into an attaché case."

"And am I delivering in town or out of town?"

"Here in town."

I pulled on my bottom lip as I gave the matter some thought.

"What's wrong?" Corky asked, then seemed annoyed with himself. Or maybe Walter Rutlidge was annoyed with his question.

"I don't know," I said. "That's a lot of money for a simple delivery. Something's not right, here."

"Do you not need five grand, son?"

"I always need money, Corky," I said, "but I prefer to earn it. This seems . . ."

"Okay," Barnes said, moving forward in his chair. He put his elbow firmly on the desk. "I'll sweeten the pot for you, a bit."

"How?"

"Corky—" Walter Rutlidge said from behind me, but Barnes waved him off.

"No, no, Walter," Barnes said. "The man obviously needs more convincin'."

"I need reasons, Corky," I said.

"More than five thousand reasons?" Walter asked.

"I'm afraid so."

"So okay," Corky said. "I hear you're tired of being just a session guy. What if I offer you a chance to record your own songs?"

"A chance?"

"You do this for me, son," Barnes said, "make this little ol' delivery, and I'll let you record a demo of your own songs."

"A demo."

"Well now, I can't rightly promise you a contract right out," Barnes argued. "I can't just hand you a deal for a CD, but I'll give you a chance. Isn't that what everybody in Nashville is looking for? A chance?"

I didn't know about *everybody* in Nashville, but it was what I'd been looking for the past eight years.

"So whataya say, son?" Corky asked. "You game?"

"I still get the five grand?" I asked.

"I'll hand you the cash when I hand you the attaché case," Corky said. "How's that for trust? You get paid even before the delivery."

"And the demo?"

"You tell me when you're ready with your songs, and we'll set it up."

I hesitated.

"You want Walter to draw up a paper?" Corky asked. "I'm a man of my word, Auggie."

He actually was. His reputation said he was a hard man, and he was slick, but when he agreed to something he followed through.

What the hell, I thought. Five grand would've been good enough, but a chance? Finally?

"Okay, Mr. Barnes," I said. "When do you want me?"

Corky Barnes looked past me again, and I heard Walter Rutlidge stand up.

"Be here tonight, Auggie," he said, coming into view. "ten P.M. We'll give you the case and tell you where to deliver it."

"You can set it up that quick?"

"If we can't, I'll call you."

I stood up. "Okay. I'll be here."

Corky stood up and stuck out his hand. "Pleasure doing business with you, son."

We shook hands firmly, and then I followed Rutlidge as he headed for the door.

"Wait a minute, wait a minute," Corky said. "I remember now."

I hoped he was wrong.

"Yeah, yeah, Velez," he said, "I remember . . . you had a song out about eight years ago. It was a hit . . . what was it . . ."

"I was just the co-writer," I said, hoping he'd get off the subject. "It wasn't much."

"It was one of them novelty songs, right?" he asked excitedly.

"I'd rather not—"

He snapped his fingers and said, "I've got it. 'Stan, Stan the Pool Man.' Right?"

I cringed. It was actually "Stan, Stan the Pool Man (or Drowning in Your Love)," but I just nodded.

"That song's been recorded a few times," Barnes said. "It was even the theme of a TV series."

"A short-lived TV series, thank God," I answered.

"It must have made you rich."

"No, like I said, I co-wrote. I do get an occasional royalty check, but I'm far from rich."

"You got any other songs like that?" he asked. "For your demo?"

"No," I said, and walked out of the office.

5

OUT IN THE RECEPTION AREA AGAIN THE GIRL LOOKED up at us as we came out.

"See you tonight, Auggie," Rutlidge said, "and I hope I don't have to tell you, discretion is also a part of this."

"Don't worry, Walter," I said. "I can keep my mouth shut."

Rutlidge nodded, and returned to Barnes' office, closing the door firmly behind him.

I looked at Allegra, who made a face like she'd just bitten into something sour.

"I know," I said, "he's pretty much of an asshole."

"Pretty much?" she asked.

"What about your boss?"

She smiled. "I'm not just another pretty face, and I sure ain't dumb enough to badmouth my boss." A Southern accent she was trying to hide managed to come out in that sentence.

DOWNSTAIRS ON THE STREET, I stopped to take the environment in. I had always loved being on Music Row. You can find hundreds of businesses connected to the music industry. Radio stations, publishing houses, music licensing firms, record labels, recording studios—where I have spent some quality time—among others.

Noshville was on Broadway and 19th Street. When I got there, Elton was already seated, with a guitar case next to him. While the ambiance was kind of antiseptic, their deli cases were not. They were filled to overflowing. We each got a sandwich on a bagel and coffee, carrying our order back to the table.

"So what happened?" he asked, excitedly.

"I got a job."

"Doin' what?"

"I can't say."

"Hey, dude, don't you trust me?"

"Sure, I do, but this is business, dude."

"All right, fine," he said, biting into his corned beef sandwich. "Don't tell me what it is."

"I won't." I chowed down on my pastrami.

WE TALKED FOR A WHILE, catching up, as it had been a few days since we'd seen each other. We usually met in local clubs like the Whiskey or the Bourbon or the Bluebird Cafe, where one of us might be performing.

We were working on our coffee refills when I told him about the possible demo.

"Oh, man, that's awesome!" he exploded. "I got some tunes for you, Auggie—"

"I have my own songs, Elton," I said, without any harshness, I hoped.

"Ah, I know that, Auggie," he said. "I'm just tryin' to horn in on your success."

"Believe me," I said, "if I ever have any success, you'll be the first I let horn in."

"So tell me, what's Corky Barnes like?"

"Well, he wanted something from me, so was real nice."

"Did he know who you are?"

"No," I said. I was going to let it drop there, but I added, "Not at first."

He smiled with unrestrained glee.

"He did, though, didn't he? He knew the song." He slapped his knee, beside himself with glee. He loved it when people remembered me for . . . the song.

"Yeah, he knew it," I said.

"Was he impressed?"

"I don't know," I said. "I left."

"Why does it bother you so much?"

"I've told you before," I said. "It was a fluke, and it was a horrible, horrible song."

"Have you heard from your co-writer?"

"No."

"Want to tell me his, or her, name?"

"No, Elton." The name on the song was a pseudonym, and the real person had never come out from behind it.

He shrugged. "Just thought I'd try again."

I'd never tell him, or anyone, who I wrote that song with. As it was, I'd never hear the end of it. That would just make it worse.

OUTSIDE OF NOSHVILLE, we split up.

"Are you going back to the studio?" I asked.

"Naw, I got a gig downtown," he said. "I gotta go home and get ready."

"Where are you playing?"

He made a face. "Nowhere, really. I mean, it's not worth mentioning."

"I could still come and support you."

"You know how you feel about your song, Auggie?" he asked.

"Yeah."

"Well, that's how I feel about this club," he said. "I don't want you to see me playing there."

"When you put it that way I understand."

"Where are you going?"

"Truth is," I said, "I've got kind of a gig myself, tonight. I also have to get ready."

6

I SPENT THE AFTERNOON WORKING ON SOME SONGS, then walked a few blocks to Varallo's, on 4th Avenue. It traces its origins back to Frank Varallo, who opened his first restaurant in 1907. His son, Frank Jr., kept the business going on Church Street until he died in 2007. The 4th Avenue location was opened by two grandsons in 1994 and still serves great chili. I had it three-ways, which includes a tamale stuffed with beef, and spaghetti. Everything is served cafeteria style, with plastic utensils. It's not a tourist place, but where the locals go, and nobody minds the plastic. The food is that good. They serve breakfast and lunch, so I just made it.

I washed it all down with a cold beer and headed back to my place. I worked the rest of the evening, then took a shower, got dressed and headed back to Starcade Records for my ten o'clock meeting. This time I drove my car, a 2002 Toyota that I've been nursing along for a few years.

PARKING ON MUSIC ROW is not hard at ten o'clock at

night. I left my car in front of the building and went inside. Before I left that afternoon, Walter Rutlidge had told me to get in the elevator and come on up at ten, so that's what I did.

As I entered Corky Barnes's office, I saw that his girl's desk was unoccupied. I took that as a sign to go right in.

"Ah, Auggie," Walter Rutlidge said, as I entered. He was standing; Corky was seated behind his desk. They were both holding glasses filled with an amber liquid. Corky had a lit cigar in the other hand and was still wearing his black cowboy hat.

"Scotch?" Rutlidge asked.

"I'm driving," I said, "although I don't know where I'm driving to."

"Have a seat, my boy," Corky said. "We'll fill you in."

I sat across from him in the same chair I'd occupied that afternoon. Rutlidge stayed just inside my peripheral vision this time.

"Ready to go?" Corky asked.

"I'm ready."

"Are you armed?" Rutlidge asked.

"What?"

"Do you have a gun?"

"I heard you," I said, "I was just wondering why I would need a gun?" I looked at Corky. "Am I gonna need a gun for this?"

"Perhaps—" Rutlidge started, but Corky cut him off.

"I don't think so, son," he said. "You look like you can handle yourself. What are you, a middleweight?"

"I go about one sixty-five."

"You'll be fine." He set the glass down, leaned over and brought an attaché case up from the floor. It was about six inches deep, dark leather, expensive looking.

"This is it," he said. "All you have to do is deliver the little ol' thing." He very nearly said "thang." I couldn't help thinking Corky's accent was put on. Maybe he thought it was good for business.

"And?"

"What do you mean, 'and'?" he asked.

"Do I get anything back?" I asked. "Like maybe payment?"

"No, no," Corky said, waving a meaty hand, "don't worry about that. Just give it to the fella, and you're done."

"What fella?"

"The man who will be waiting for you," Rutlidge said.

"Do I get to know his name?"

"Not important." Corky picked up his glass again. I wondered why Scotch drinkers so often matched their drinks with cigars. "Just deliver the case and you're done." He opened the top drawer of his desk, choosing to once again put down the drink rather than the cigar. He took out a brown envelope and dropped it on the desk. "There's your five grand."

I left the envelope where it was. I was interested in the attaché case, wondering if it was locked.

"Where is this pass supposed to take place?" I asked.

"The Bridge," Corky said.

"The" Bridge in Nashville was the Shelby Street Bridge. Once open to traffic, it had been closed when it became a hazard. But instead of tearing it down the town fathers decided to make the 102- year-old structure into a pedestrian bridge. It opened in 2003 and was good for two things: one, it offered a good view of the Nashville skyline, and two, it allowed easy access from downtown to LP Park, where the NFL Titans played their games.

"What time?"

"Midnight."

"Which side?"

"The other side."

The local government considered the bridge to be a tourist attraction, but both sides of the bridge were kind of iffy in the off season, and after dark. I could have walked it from my place, but it was a long hike in the dark, and you were asking for trouble.

I'd have to drive there and then walk across it for the meet. The bridge itself was lit at night, but maybe I did need a gun.

"Why all the cloak-and-dagger stuff, Corky?" I asked. "Why don't I just meet this dude at the Whiskey and give him the case? Good food, great music—"

"He wants it this way," Walter Rutlidge said. "He's calling the shots, Auggie."

I pointed to the case. "This is not a blackmail payoff, is it?"

"No," Rutlidge said, "it's nothing like that."

"There's no money inside," Corky said, putting his hand on it. "I swear to you."

"Is this illegal?"

Barnes made a face.

Rutlidge said, "We're not asking you to do anything illegal, Auggie. You're just delivering the case to a man."

"A man whose name I don't get to know."

"Right."

"How will I recognize him?"

"Well," Rutlidge said, "he'll be standing at the other end of the bridge, waiting."

"Some people do walk across that bridge at night, Walter," I said. "What if I hand this case to the wrong guy?"

Corky and Walter Rutlidge exchanged a glance.

"You didn't think of that?" I asked.

"He . . . he'll just be standing at the far end of the bridge, waiting," Rutlidge said.

"Maybe he could wear an overcoat and a fedora," I suggested.

"In Indian Summer?" Barnes asked.

"I was being facetious. Can you get hold of him? Cell phone?"

Barnes looked at Walter, who said, "Yes."

"Just call him," I said, standing up. I put my hand on the attaché case, picked up the envelope with the other. "Tell him to say . . . 'Titans' to me so I know who he is."

"What will you say to him?"

". . . touchdown," I answered after a pause, feeling silly.

I looked at my watch. It was ten-thirty. I could actually get there ahead of him and be waiting. I suggested this out loud.

"No!" Corky said. "He was very specific. Y'all are to walk across that bridge at midnight, boy. He'll be waiting."

I nodded.

"You sure you don't want a gun?" Walter Rutlidge asked.

"I don't want a gun, Walter," I said. "But give me the guy's phone number. Just in case."

Reluctantly he did.

7

I TRIED TO THINK OF A WAY TO KILL TIME, BUT everything I thought of involved clubs and music and drinking. I didn't want to do that while I had five grand in my pocket and an attaché filled with who-knew-what. In the end, I drove downtown to 1st and Broadway and sat in the car for a while, worked on some songs in my head.

When it was time, I drove down the street to a 1st Avenue 24-hour parking lot. I thought about leaving the car on the street somewhere but decided against it.

The darkened park had seen plenty of action over the years, from concerts, fireworks displays and fairs. It also housed Fort Nashborough, a replica of the original fort that was built along the Cumberland in 1870.

It was quiet and deserted as I walked through to the bridge, except for a young couple getting to know one another a little better.

I had debated what to do with the money. I could have driven home and left it there, but that would have given me another decision—take the car or walk back? Besides, I liked the way the envelope felt in the pocket of my jeans, folded in half and shoved down there. Leaving it in the car wasn't an option, either. That would have made me nervous. And I was nervous enough, Which was why I had the tire iron from the trunk in my back pocket, covered with my Jimi Hendrix T-shirt. Jimi was rocking out on his Stratocaster.

When I got to the entrance of the bridge, I looked around, didn't see anybody. I looked across to the other end, but that was about 3,000 feet away and it was dark. I couldn't see a thing.

There were some lights on the bridge, but they weren't very bright. I walked along, kept my eye on the glittering skyline. The attaché case started to get heavier in my hand.

In the car, I had tried the catches on the case, but they were locked as I expected. I thought about forcing it open so I could really see what I'd gotten myself into, but I didn't. I'd given my word.

I could hear my footsteps on the bridge; it was that quiet. The night was still, warm and sticky, but that wasn't the only reason I was sweating. As I got closer to the other side, I could make out LP Park in the distance, totally dark, and I started thinking about the gun Walter had offered me. Would Mike Hammer be taking this walk without a gun?

Then I started to think about Big'n'Rich's "Ride a Horse, Save a Cowboy" video, which had been shot entirely on this bridge, and I was less nervous. I started to sing it to myself and forgot about needing a gun, or a tire iron. Music always made me feel better.

Finally, I saw a figure. At first, it didn't move, but then I saw the glowing end of a cigarette. In a few seconds, the smoke made its way over to me.

I slowed down as I approached. There was a sliver of a moon that wasn't helping very much, but I was pretty sure it was just him and me on that bridge.

When I got to within three feet of him, I could smell his cologne, but still couldn't see his features because he was wearing a hoodie with the hood up. His face was in the shadows. However, I could tell that he was under six feet tall and slender. And still. He stood very still.

I stopped.

"You got something for me?" he asked, the voice coming out of the darkness hoarsely.

I squinted, still trying to make out his face, but I couldn't. It was as if he was faceless.

"Have you got something to say to me?"

"Fuck," he said, beneath his breath. I saw the cigarette go flying into the Cumberland River. Then he said, "Titans."

"Touchdown."

"They aren't a very good team, are they?" he drawled. I got the feeling the rough quality to his voice was an attempt at disguising it.

"I wouldn't know, dude," I said. "I'm not a football fan."

"Me, neither," the man said. "That case mine?"

"Yeah," I said, "yeah, it's yours."

"Give it here."

He put his right hand out. I saw a cat's eye ring on the third finger. I reached out and handed him the case. He took the handle from me.

"Turn around and start walking back," he said.

"Aren't you going to—"

"Open it? No, not here," he said, laughing. "Your boss knows better than to fuck me on this." Then he laughed some more, only this time it sounded mean. "At least, he better know that. Go on, walk away. I wanna watch you leave before I do."

I remembered what Walter said about him calling the shots, so I turned and started walking back across the bridge. When I stopped to turn around and look, he was gone.

8

Back to the present . . .

I TOLD THE DETECTIVES EVERYTHING.

"So that was it?" Hollinger said.

"That was it," I said. "I continued to my side of the bridge, got my car out of the parking lot, and went home."

"That's not everything," Lewis said. "The next day you deposited five thousand dollars in your account."

"Forty-eight hundred, actually," I corrected him. "I kept two hundred out for pocket money."

"Forty-eight hundred," Lewis repeated.

"The money you say Corky Barnes paid you."

"Not the money I *say* he paid me," I said. "The money he paid me."

"And who was present when he paid you?" Hollinger asked.

"Just Me, Corky Barnes and the lawyer, Walter Rutlidge."

"And does anyone else know about your appointment with Barnes?"

"Well . . . there was Barnes's secretary," I said.

"What's her name?" Hollinger asked, opening his notepad.

"I don't know . . . Allegra," I said. "Walter Rutlidge called her Allegra."

He wrote down her name. At least, I assumed he was writing down her name.

"Anyone else?"

I hesitated, then said, "Elton."

"Who's Elton?"

"He's a friend of mine."

"Where can we find him?"

I gave them his address and phone number, hoping I'd be able to get to him before they did and warn him.

"And he was there?" he asked, writing.

"Well, no," I said, "but I saw him just before I went to the meeting. Remember, I told you about the session."

He ignored the comment. "So he knew you were going there. Did you see him after?"

"Yes," I said, "I told you, we had lunch together."

"And you had the attaché case with you?" Lewis asked.

"No, I told you," I said, "they gave it to me that night. Detective, I think maybe it's time I knew what was going on."

Hollinger closed his notebook.

"We'll get to that, trust me," Hollinger said. "Do you still claim you don't know Felix Nolan?"

"I never heard of Felix Nolan."

"Six feet tall, lots of black hair, kinda ugly . . ." Hollinger said, trying to be helpful.

Tall, I thought, black hair . . .

"Wait a minute," I said. "Does he wear a cat's eye ring on his right hand?"

"Cat's eye—"

"Yeah," Lewis said, "yeah, that's what the M.E. said it was. A cat's eye ring."

Hollinger looked at his partner, and then back at me.

"So you did know him?"

"Did?" I asked.

"He's dead," Hollinger said. "Felix Nolan is dead."

"Oh. How did he die?"

"He was killed," Lewis said. "Shot."

"And you did know him," Hollinger said, pursuing his point.

"No," I said, "but I think . . . the guy I gave the attaché case to, he was about six feet tall, and he wore a cat's eye ring."

"Would you know him if you saw him again?"

"No," I said, "I never saw his face. Whatever made you think I knew him?"

"He had a piece of paper in his pocket," Hollinger said. "It had your name on it, and the word 'Titan.'"

"Titan?"

He nodded.

Okay, I hadn't told him about "Titan" and "Touchdown," because I thought it was silly, so I told them about it.

"Code words?" Lewis asked.

"I know, it was silly, but I don't do this very often," I said. "I thought I needed a way to identify him before I gave him the case."

"The attaché case you never opened," Lewis said.

"That's right."

"But you tried?"

"I just tried the catches, but they were locked."

"Was it heavy?" Hollinger asked.

"It was . . . like, normal. I mean, it didn't feel like it had rocks in it, or anything. Just maybe some . . . papers."

"Rattle?" Hollinger asked.

"Huh?"

"Did anything rattle around inside when you shook it?"

"I never shook it."

"I woulda shook it," Lewis said. "But that's just me. I'm curious."

"Must be why you became a detective," I said. I looked at Hollinger. "So I'm here because you found my name in his pocket?"

"Yes."

"Well," I said, "I think I explained that to you. Corky Barnes, or Walter Rutlidge, must have given him my name after I agreed to meet him."

"Could be."

"What else could it be?"

"I don't know," Hollinger said. "That's why I'm asking questions because I'm a detective. I'm trying to detect."

"I think you should be detecting somewhere else," I said. "How about talking to Barnes or Rutlidge?"

"We did talk to them," Lewis said.

"You did?"

"Yeah," Hollinger said. "They said they never heard of Felix Nolan."

"You know what else?" Lewis asked, coming closer and leaning over me. "Neither one of them said anything about hiring you."

9

"WHAT?"

"Not a peep," Hollinger said. "Why do you think that is, Auggie?"

"Just off the top of my head," I said, "maybe they have something to hide."

"Or you do," Hollinger said.

"I've told you everything I can," I said. "Everything I know."

"Are you sure?"

"Yup. Did you ask Corky why the dead man had his name in his pocket?"

"He said maybe the guy was a musician. Lots of musicians carry his name."

"Along with mine?"

"He's got no explanation for that."

"He wouldn't."

"Tell me something," Hollinger said. "When you parked that night, did you get a ticket? Or a receipt?"

"A ticket," I said. "I got a ticket when I drove in."

"Did you keep it?"

"I don't know."

"You said you self-parked," Lewis said. "You wouldn't need the ticket to get out, then."

"Maybe . . ." I said, taking my wallet out of my pocket. They had checked me for weapons but hadn't taken anything off me.

I checked my wallet, didn't find it there. Usually, I have some bank receipts, some credit card receipts folded up, but before I leave town—like to go on tour—I usually clean out my wallet and throw everything into a drawer. I did find a woman's name and a phone number. On one of our stops, there were some cougars in the audience who came backstage. One of them was a brunette about forty, with heavy breasts in a tank top, nipples on display beneath the thin fabric. Yeah, okay, I couldn't resist. I woke up with her name and number on the table next to the bed. I put it back in my wallet.

"I don't have it."

"Look around at home," Hollinger said. "It might help you."

"Help me?" I asked, putting my wallet away. "You don't really suspect me of this, do you?"

"He did have your name on him," Lewis pointed out.

"We'll be checking things out, Auggie," Hollinger said. "That ticket would help."

"And while you're at it," I suggested, "how about talking to Barnes and Rutlidge again and asking them point blank if they hired me?"

"We know how to do our jobs," Lewis said.

"You could've fooled me," I said. "Why didn't you just tell me in the beginning that his guy was dead? Instead of playing games?"

"We're not playing, Auggie," Hollinger said, standing up. "The sooner you realize that, the better."

"Just because we've been nice doesn't mean we're playin'," Lewis said.

"Sit tight," Hollinger said, as they both headed for the door.

"Hey, I'm still not under arrest, right?"

"That's right," Hollinger said. "You're just here for an interview."

They left. If they weren't lying, I'd be out in an hour or so. Then maybe I could ask Barnes and Rutlidge some questions of my own.

WHEN THE DOOR opened again half an hour later, Hollinger was there alone.

"Come on," he said, "I'll give you a ride home."

I stood up and said, "I can walk."

"Don't cop an attitude, Auggie," Hollinger said. "Come on."

I relented and let him drive me home.

In the car, he said, "That's quite a collection of guitars you've got at your place."

He'd said that before. Why bring it up again, I wondered.

"You play?"

"I'm something of a three-cord idiot," he said. "Played when I was a kid, didn't keep it up. Still got a guitar of my own, but nothing like what you've got."

"You should've seen what I was playing on tour," I told him and explained about the access I'd had to all the instruments that belonged to the guy I was replacing.

I knew what he was doing, being a nice guy to lull me

into a false sense of security. I made sure I didn't talk about anything but guitars for the short ride.

He pulled up in front of my place and cut the engine.

"This is a good club?" he asked.

"The Bourbon is one of the best."

I started to open the door to get out, but he put his hand on my arm.

"How long were you gone on this tour?" he asked.

"Two weeks."

"Short tour."

"As I said, I was replacing someone."

"On a Gretchen Wilson tour?"

"It was a favor," I said. "I'm usually more of a Big'n'Rich kind of guy."

"I'm an Alison Krauss and Union Station guy, myself."

That explained a lot, I thought.

"Can I go now?" I asked.

"Yeah," he said, "just don't go on any tours in the near future."

"I just got back," I said. "I need some rest."

"Good," Hollinger said. "I wouldn't want to have to come looking for you."

"I'll be around," I said, opening the door. "I don't have any reason to leave town."

"That's good to hear."

I started to get out again, then stopped and looked back at him.

"What was in the attaché case?" I asked.

"We don't know," he said. "We never found it."

I got out, slammed the door, and he took off. I went back upstairs, feeling even more ragged than when I had gotten off the bus. The situation called for some thought, but my brain was mush. I needed sleep before I could concentrate on my predicament.

10

As soon as I got upstairs, I fell onto the bed and into a dreamless sleep. When I woke, I was hungry—too hungry to take the time to shower, dress and decide what restaurant to go to. My one big weakness is that I love Nashville restaurants. There are so many good ones I often have trouble picking one out. But in this case, I opted for a couple of English muffins with butter and jelly and coffee. Add a glass of O.J., and the breakfast taxed my talents as a chef.

I ate my muffins, drank my juice, and then walked around the loft with a second cup of coffee and a guitar around my neck, this time my Fender. I was waiting for my brain to wake up enough to concentrate on what the cops had told me.

I walked past my guitars, some of which were on Hercules stands. They were all acoustic; the Taylor 710CE, the Takamine, and the Little Martin were the ones I used the most. I hadn't bought any of them new, but they were among the finest used ones I'd ever seen. There was an empty stand on the end — the Fender that was around my neck.

I took my coffee over to one of the front windows and stared down at Printers Alley. The thing I had noticed about the Alley from the first day I moved in was there's always music coming from somewhere. At night it came from the clubs, but during the day it was just in the air. Whether it was somebody with their radio on and window open, or street musicians who were playing on the corner, it was always there, because that was Nashville. They didn't call it Music City for nothing. The heart and soul of Nashville was music.

But at that moment the music was coming from across the street, the second floor. I knew there were a couple of young musicians living there who had moved in recently. They practiced morning and afternoons. I assumed they went out nights and played somewhere. We hadn't met yet, so all I knew was what I saw—and heard. They weren't very good, but give them credit; they kept practicing.

When I'd finished the coffee, I took the cup to the sink, then walked to the studio end of the loft. Gently I lifted the Fender from my neck, set it on its stand, then stared at it. My favorite—I took it everywhere.

I'd acquired that guitar during my tour of duty in Afghanistan. It was there I had met Jimmy Quinn, who taught me how to play the thing. Jimmy, Terry Jansen and I had formed a trio during the time we served together, and were determined to go "on the road" when we got back home, and make a name for ourselves.

Yeah, that was the plan . . .

IT WAS NOVEMBER 13, 2001 when the Marines marched

into Kabul. Actually, we trudged in. The town had already fallen to a Northern Alliance aerial bombardment and all that was left were craters, burned out buildings, and abandoned Taliban guns.

We were there as part of Operation Enduring Freedom, which was launched after 9-11. The Fall of Kabul was a major blow to the Taliban. By November 16th the Taliban had been forced to retreat back to Kandahar, where they belonged.

We were tired when we got there, but we still had to spend the next half hour cleaning out a group of Taliban fighters who had taken refuge in the city park.

After that was done, we took off our helmets, lit up cigarettes and Jimmy broke out the guitar while we waited for further orders. Jimmy took flak for carrying the guitar everywhere, but he strapped it to his back and never let it get in his way during the action.

Jimmy was playing the Fender, Terry his mouth organ. I'd never learned how to sing harmony, but I was always able to find it, so when Jimmy started singing, I'd chime in. A few of the other boys gathered around to listen to us sing and play. It wasn't smart, so many American and British soldiers in one place, as well as Freedom Fighters. But we had cleaned the place out and were feeling good.

It was the last time I ever did that.

There may have been a crowd around us, but there was room for one bullet, one lone sniper bullet, to make its way through and hit Jimmy right in the back of the head. He fell forward, the Fender hitting the ground next to him.

We grabbed up our rifles and riddled the sniper with bullets. He fell from the rooftop he'd been hiding on, dead before he hit the ground. He'd fired one shot, and it had killed Jimmy.

A few of the boys lifted his body to carry it to safety— too little, too late. I picked the Fender up off the ground, his blood still on it.

I WIPED AWAY a tear and turned from the Fender. I'd wiped his blood off it that day, but it still bore the scars of the Afghan conflict, as did I.

Terry and I, we had almost been court-martialed for that incident. No more guitars, no more jam sessions on the battlefield after that, and we saved our singing for more appropriate places.

It was time to get dressed—Eric Clapton on the shirt, this time, caressing his 1964 Cherry-Red Gibson ES-335 — time to address the problems at hand, and not to dwell on the problems of the past.

11

CORKY BARNES AND WALTER RUTLIDGE HAD HIRED ME to deliver an attaché case to a man whose name they wouldn't divulge. They'd assured me there was nothing illegal involved. No, check that. They'd told me I wouldn't be doing anything illegal, which was a very different thing.

Had they lied to me, and made me deliver a load of drugs?

The cops didn't know what was in the case. They hadn't seen it. They'd found the body of Felix Nolan, days after he and I had "met"—(how many days? I'd never asked) so why wouldn't he still have the case with him?

Not only had I not asked when they found him, but where. And who said that the attaché case I'd handed him had anything to do with his murder? Maybe it was something else entirely? And he just happened to have my name in his pocket still? That part bothered me. And the part about Barnes and Rutlidge not telling the cops they'd paid me five thousand dollars.

Hell, even to me that sounded like a drug deal.

· · ·

I CALLED Elton and told him to meet me in the park, by Bradley's statue. He knew most of what had happened before I went on tour. Now that I was back I was going to need him to back me up.

When I got to the park, no one was by the statue, not Jasmine performing her horrible songs, and not Elton. But no sooner had I turned around when I saw him walking towards me.

"Hey, hey, my favorite country picker. How was the tour?"

"It was good," I said. "Went real well."

He shook his head. "You and Gretchen Wilson. That's a match made in heaven. You get any?"

"I was working, Elton," I said, "and she's a professional."

"Yeah, a hot professional."

"Hey, I got paid. That's why I was there. That, and it was a favor."

"How much?"

"How much what?"

"How much didja get paid?"

"None of your business, dude."

"Enough to buy me lunch again?"

"Sure," I said, "but let's talk first. Over here." I walked him to a bench and we sat. It was odd that neither one of us was holding a guitar.

"What's up?"

I told him about the detectives picking me up soon after I arrived home, explained the how and why of their interest.

"And this has something to do with Starcade Records and Corky Barnes?"

"It might," I said, "but even if it doesn't, they're gonna want to question you."

"About what?"

"About that day," I said, "the day I went to see Barnes. How I played a session with you just before and then had lunch with you after."

"Well, okay . . . what do you want me to tell them?"

"The truth," I said. "Just tell them when we saw each other and what we talked about."

"What did we talk about, exactly?" he asked. "I'm not sure I remember. Maybe you should refresh my memory. What was it you were doing for Starcade Records?"

He was fishing for more info. I considered not telling him, then decided, what the hell? I needed him to back my story, so I might as well keep him happy.

"I was making a delivery," I said.

"Of what?"

"I don't know, but it was in an attaché case, which I handed to a dude who later turned up dead."

"Wow," he said. "Just like a real private eye."

"You mean just like a fictional private eye, don't you?"

"Whatever," he said. "Did they show you the dead guy?"

"Yeah, but there was no point," I said. "I never saw the guy's face."

"So then, you don't know if the dead guy really is the same one you gave the case to, do you?"

"Actually, no. Since I've been away for two weeks, I'm not even sure how long he's been dead. But they found my name on a piece of paper in his pocket."

"Why would he have that?"

"One of two reasons," I said. "Either Barnes and

Rutlidge gave my name to him, and he just left it in his pocket."

"Or?"

"Or somebody's trying to set me up."

"Who?"

"I don't know," I said, "but according to the cops, Barnes and Rutlidge didn't tell them they hired me to do anything. So they're wondering where I got the money I put in my bank."

"Money? How much?"

"A lot."

"Come on! You've told me everything else, Auggie," he pleaded. "Why y'all holdin' out on me now, dude?"

"Five grand."

"Wow," he said, again. "Wait a minute. They don't think you gave the dead guy the case and *he* paid you, do they? Like a drug deal?"

"You're a smart cookie."

"You mean, smarter than I look?" he asked. "Or smarter than you thought I was."

"Neither one," I said. "I'm your friend, remember? I know you're smart."

"The cops'll think I'm dumb," he predicted.

"Why?"

He shrugged. "Citizens think musicians are dumb."

"That's not true."

"Well . . . I get treated that way."

Elton didn't look dumb, he just looked . . . strange. The way he dressed could be called second-hand chic, and he was tall—real tall, and thin. And he wore very thick glasses. Still, I don't see why anyone would just assume he was dumb, but who was I to argue with his experience?

"They'll believe what you tell them."

"I'll tell them the truth."

"That's all I need."

"I think you need more than that," he said. "I think you need Mr. Corky Barnes and his lawyer to back your story."

"I do," I said, "and I'm on my way to make sure they do."

"Lunch after?" he asked.

"I'll give you a rain check," I said. "Why don't you go home so the cops can find you when they want to?"

"Yeah, okay," he said, "but call me later and let me know what's goin' on, okay?"

"Okay." I stood up. "Later."

12

I'D GIVEN THE SITUATION A LOT OF THOUGHT THAT morning and had just talked the whole thing out with Elton. Now I needed to talk to Corky Barnes and Walter Rutlidge to find out what the hell was going on. Even if Felix Nolan's death had nothing to do with the attaché case, I still needed them to vouch for my story with the cops.

Walking from the park to Starcade Records I realized I hadn't acted like any kind of private eye with the cops. I hadn't asked the questions I should have asked. Consequently, I didn't know where or when Felix Nolan had been killed.

I entered the building and had to stop at the security desk to present myself to the hulking guard. I guess Corky Barnes liked to pretend he was in New York or L.A.

"Auggie Velez to see Mr. Barnes," I said. "Or Mr. Rutlidge."

"You got an appointment?" he asked.

"No," I said, "but I think they'll see me. Unless they want to see the police, instead."

"Police?"

"Just call," I said, pointing to the phone.

He looked like he wanted to throw me out on my ass, but instead picked up the phone and made the call.

When he hung up he said, "Go on up."

"Thanks."

I rode the elevator impatiently. When the door opened Rutlidge was standing there. Last time his suit had been blue. This time brown. I knew he had an office downtown —or, at least, he used to.

"Hello, Auggie."

"You sonofabitch," I said.

He put his hands up in a defensive pose and said, "I understand why you're upset."

"I want to talk to Barnes, and you." I stepped out of the elevator, and the doors closed behind me.

"Corky's not—"

"Don't tell me he's not in the office," I said. "He doesn't go anywhere, does he? Unless he has to? At least, that's what everybody says."

"Well, yes, but—"

"He's in the building," I said. "Get him. Or I'll talk to the cops."

"You've already talked to the cops, I'm sure."

"True," I said, "but I might have a lot more to say."

"Okay," Rutlidge said, "okay, take it easy. Come with me."

I followed him down a hall, past Corky Barnes's office. The door was open, and I saw a girl sitting at the desk in there. It wasn't Allegra, the girl I'd seen last time.

Rutlidge took me to another office, one with no secretary.

"Wait here," he said. "I'll find Corky."

"What happened to Allegra?"

"Who?" He looked at me, genuinely puzzled.

"Allegra," I said. "Corky's secretary."

"Oh, her," Rutlidge said. "She, uh, left."

"She left, or was replaced?"

"I don't know," he said. "Corky doesn't check with me before he fires or hires. Wait here; I'll be right back."

He left. I looked at a door I thought connected this office to Corky's, thought about going through and talking to the girl at the desk. She wasn't there that night, but maybe she knew what had happened to Allegra.

I decided against it for the moment. Fist I needed to have a good talk with Barnes and Rutlidge.

I was surprised when Rutlidge came through the connecting door.

"Okay, Auggie," Rutlidge said. "Let's go see Mr. Barnes."

I followed Rutlidge into the other office, past the receptionist. She didn't even look up, but I could see she wasn't as pretty as Allegra.

We went into Corky's office. He was seated behind his desk, decked out in his hat and cigar, his dark western style suit. A diamond ring sparkled on each hand today.

"Auggie, my boy," he said, expansively, "nice to see you again."

"Maybe it won't be so nice."

Rutlidge closed the door behind us.

"Have a seat, Auggie," Rutlidge said, "and don't be so aggressive."

"Why not?" I asked. "You two hung me out to dry with the cops."

"I don't know what you mean by that, son," Corky said.

"They talked to you about Felix Nolan being murdered, and you never told them about hiring me."

"It wasn't any of their business," Corky said. "Besides, they never did ask."

"And now I'm a suspect in the murder of Felix Nolan," I said.

"I'm sorry for that, I truly am, but—" Corky started, but I didn't let him get any further.

"You guys have to tell the cops you paid me that five thousand dollars," I said. "Right now they think I sold Nolan something, like drugs."

"We can't do that—" Corky started, but I cut him off again, because I still wasn't hearing that I wanted to hear.

"You sure as hell can!" I shouted.

"Look, Auggie," Walter Rutlidge said, "we had nothing to do with Nolan being killed—"

"Well, neither did I."

"We understand that," Rutlidge said. "Do the police have that attaché case?"

"How should I know?"

"Could they have it?" Barnes asked.

"I guess," I said, "but I doubt it."

"Why?" Rutlidge asked.

"Because if they had it, they wouldn't suspect me of selling something illegal." I looked at both of them. "Unless there *was* something?"

"No," Corky insisted, "there weren't nothin' illegal."

"Well," I asked, "what *was* in it, then?"

Corky looked at Rutlidge. It was as if the two men were of one mind, and had come to some agreement without speaking.

"We can't tell you that," Rutlidge said.

"Damn it, Walter!" I said. "I'm not taking the fall for five thousand—"

"Don't forget your demo boy," Corky said, cutting me off this time.

"Fuck the demo," I said. "I won't be able to record from prison. Look, either you guys help me out, or I'll throw you to the cops."

"Whataya mean by that?" Barnes asked.

"I'll tell them you wanted me to kill Nolan, and I refused," I told him. "I'll suggest maybe you hired somebody else to do it, or worse, maybe you did it yourselves."

Corky laughed uncomfortably.

"They'll never believe that," he said. He looked at Rutlidge. "Will they?"

"It might start them thinking," Rutlidge said.

"Okay," Corky said. "Okay."

"Okay, you'll tell them?" I demanded.

"I mean, okay," Corky said, "let's try to work something out, here."

"Don't offer me more money," I said. "I can't use money in prison any more than I could a contract with you."

"You know," Corky said, "we *could* record you from prison. It would be a great—"

"Corky," Rutlidge said.

Corky stopped talking.

13

WE ALL SAT DOWN.

"Let's talk this over calmly," Rutlidge said.

"I'm plumb calm," Corky said.

He wasn't, though. He wanted to pretend like I was the only one who was upset, but I didn't like being the only one, so I was going to do my best to pass it on until they agreed to help me.

But I could do it calmly, I decided.

"Nolan was killed only a few days after you made the delivery," Rutlidge said. He put his right hand up, palm out. "I swear we had nothing to do with it."

"But it does have something to do with the attaché case, right?"

"We think so. Then again there's always a chance it doesn't. He could have gotten somebody else mad enough to kill him."

"So how do we know for sure?" I asked.

"We need to get that case back," Rutlidge said.

"After two weeks? Who the hell knows where that thing is? It could be anywhere."

"We want you to find it."

"Without knowing what's in it?"

Neither of them answered.

"You won't clear me without it?"

"We can be stubborn," Rutlidge said.

"Even if I toss a suggestion into the cop's ear?"

"I still think they'll figure you're better for it than we are. You want to take that chance?" the lawyer asked.

"What do I get out of it?" I asked.

"Another five grand," Corky said.

"Corky!" Rutlidge barked.

"It's only money," Corky said, with a shrug.

"And a recording contract," Rutlidge said.

Corky looked at him now.

"Guaranteed," Rutlidge added.

"Yeah," Corky said, looking at me, "yeah, guaranteed."

So all I had to do was find an attaché case, stay clear of a murder charge, and I'd get my chance.

I didn't know a musician who wouldn't have taken that deal.

"I'll need to know where this Nolan lived," I said, "and anything else you can tell me about him."

"Walter can help you with that," Corky said. "I've got a conference call."

"I'm gonna want to get paid today," I said. "In advance."

"Walter can take care of that, too," Corky said,

"Okay," Rutlidge said, standing up. "Let's go to my office."

He and I stood up. I looked at Corky.

"One more thing."

"What's that, son?" he asked.

"I want to know where Allegra is."

"Who?"

"Allegra," I said. "The girl who was working at the front desk last time I was here."

"Oh, her."

"What happened to her?"

"She was . . . reassigned."

"Where?"

Corky looked at Rutlidge yet again.

"Yeah, okay," Rutlidge said. "I can help with that, too. Come on."

I followed him back out through the connecting door. His girl still didn't look at me.

In Rutlidge's office, I sat down while he opened a wall safe. He took out five grand, put it in an envelope, and handed it to me.

"What about the information on Nolan? And Allegra?"

"I'll write it down," he said, pulling a yellow pad over in front of him. "You're going to love this part."

"What part?"

He looked up at me. "He was a musician, too."

"Working?"

"Not so much."

He finished writing, tore off the page and handed it to me.

"I'll need all your phone numbers," I said, "and when I call, you better answer."

14

I LEFT STARCADE RECORDS, WAS WALKING DOWN THE street when my cell phone rang. A real ring. I didn't go in for those fancy tones. I respected my music too much. The last thing I ever wanted to hear was a Beatles song being used as a damned ringtone.

"Hello?"

"Auggie, dude, it's me." Elton.

"You okay?"

"I'm fine, dude," he said. "I talked to those detectives and told them everything I knew like you wanted me to. Man, what a couple of stiffs."

"Good man. Thanks."

"I hope it helps you."

"It can't hurt."

"What happened with Barnes?" he asked.

"Well," I said, "that didn't exactly go as planned."

I ran it down real quick for him, promised I'd tell him the whole story when I saw him.

"Yeah, but are they gonna help you with the cops?" he asked.

"They will, yeah," I said, "but first I've got to do some things."

"Like what?"

"I'll tell you later, Elton," I said. "I've got to go."

"Okay, but call me, dude."

I broke the connection. I didn't want to tell him I was working for them again, didn't want to explain about the recording contract—the carrot at the end of the stick —even though I knew he, of all people, would understand. Elton was satisfied with his career, enjoyed doing session and backup work. He would have liked to get some of his songs recorded, but he wasn't interested in an album of his own. But he understood about those who were.

I had driven to Music Row, so I walked to my car, which I'd left by the park. I wanted to drive back to my place, get my bearings before I started looking for that damn case.

I realized during the drive home that in searching for the case, I might also be searching for the killer of Felix Nolan. But there was that carrot again and whoever killed him was long gone.

Or so I kept telling myself.

WHEN I GOT HOME, I stashed the second payment inside an empty guitar case. That was my safe. I might have made a little hidey-hole beneath the floorboards, but I didn't want to damage the hardwood floors.

Once again I tucked away forty-eight hundred and kept two in my wallet for walking around money. I still had a few thousand left in the bank from the original five grand. I also had a check folded in my wallet; my pay for the two weeks I was on tour. For a change I was solvent, maybe even flush.

I got a bottle of Dos Perros Ale from the frig, a product of Nashville's own Yazoo Brewing Company, and sat down with the page of information Walter Rutlidge had given me on Felix Nolan. It was basic stuff: he was thirty-eight years old, a musician (guitar and piano), and lived in Germantown, which wasn't very far. If Rutlidge knew more about the guy, he hadn't shared that info.

I was about to turn on my laptop to see if I could find anything more on the web when there was a knock. I decided I better start keeping that downstairs door locked, except that the employees of the Bourbon downstairs also used it.

I opened the door. Detective Hollinger raised his eyebrows at me.

"Where's your partner?" I asked.

"We split up, sometimes," he said. "Can I come in?"

"Can I say no?"

He didn't answer. I backed away and let him enter.

"You got another one of those?" he asked, indicating the bottle in my hand.

"Sure thing," I went to the fridge and got it, handed it to him.

"Thanks." He took a deep pull, then smacked his lips. "Never too early for a good brew."

"What can I do for you, Detective?"

"I just have a couple more questions, if you don't mind."

"I guess not."

"We've been at kind of a standstill with you out of town," he admitted. "Now we're trying to make up for lost time."

"Well, I'm all yours."

"We talked to your friend," he said, cutting me off before I could protest. "He backs your story."

"I knew he would."

"Because you coached him?"

"I didn't have to. He's honest."

"Kind of a flake, though, huh?"

"An honest flake."

He took my place in at a glance. "Mind if I walk around?"

"You trying to do a search, Detective?" I asked. "Without a warrant?"

"Do I need a warrant?"

I didn't answer.

"Okay, look, I'm just curious. I just want to walk over there and look at your axes."

"Go ahead."

I decided to walk along with him.

"So, how long you been playing?" he asked.

"About ten years," I said.

"Really? That's all? I thought you were going to say that you started taking lessons when you were ten, or something like that."

"Never really had any lessons."

"You're self-taught?"

"Not exactly."

We reached the guitars, each upright on its stand.

"Well, if you never took lessons and you're not self-taught, then how do you know how to play?"

"I served with a guy in Afghanistan," I said. "He showed me some chords, and I took it from there."

"So you're a natural."

I shrugged. "That's what some people say."

"What about singing? Do you sing?"

"I can carry a tune."

"Have you made any records?"

"I've been on recordings," I said. "Singing backup, and harmony."

"Harmony," he said. "Now there's something I don't understand. How do you know how to sing harmony?"

"I can just . . . hear it," I said. "Always could."

Hollinger shook his head and said, "A natural."

He crouched down in front of my kids. "This is a used Takamine, isn't it?"

"That's right." I'd bought that one with my first royalty check from "the song." Okay, yeah, so maybe that makes me a whore.

"And that's a Taylor? Also used?"

"You know your axes." A friend of mine had given me the Taylor about fours years earlier when I turned thirty.

He stood up, drank his beer. "I told you, I play a little."

"Maybe we should play together," I said, "after you're sure I'm not a killer, that is."

"Yeah," he said, "after that." He finished the beer and handed me the bottle. "Thanks for the drink. I'll be on my way, now."

"You get what you wanted?" I asked.

He studied me for a moment, then said, "I think so."

I walked him to the door, setting his empty bottle aside on a table.

"Have you talked to Barnes and Rutlidge yet?" I asked.

"I'm gonna do that later today. Why, did you coach them, too?"

"I haven't coached anybody," I said. "Remember?"

"Do you think they'll tell me the truth?"

"Probably not."

"Why not?"

"They're record execs," I said. "They're not used to telling the truth."

"Why do you want to be part of this industry, then?"

"I like playing music," I said, "I like writing songs. Seems only natural to try and get paid for it."

"You write songs, too?"

Damn, I thought, shouldn't have told me that. If he looked me up, he was going to find "the song."

"A few."

"Anything I'd know?"

"Probably not."

He studied me again. I think he was curious to see if I'd balk at letting him "walk around," as if I had something to hide. Maybe he was satisfied that I didn't. Not here, anyway.

"Thanks again, Auggie," he said. "For the beer, I mean."

"Sure."

"And the offer to play," he added. "Maybe I'll take you up on it . . . later."

I closed the door behind him, listened as he trudged down the stairs. If Hollinger was the good cop, that would make Lewis the bad cop. I wondered when *he'd* make *his* move.

PART 2

Flauntin' It (Don't Mean You Wear It Well)

Augusto Velez-Colon

15

AFTER HOLLINGER LEFT I POPPED THE CAP ON ANOTHER beer and fired up my laptop. Over the last few years, since acquiring my private investigator's license, I had also acquired specialized knowledge enabling me to run an investigation into someone's background online. Then there were contacts which scored me some passwords, allowing me to get into websites that otherwise would have been closed to me.

I was able to check Felix Nolan's credit score and report. While I'd seen worse, Nolan's numbers would not have allowed him to buy a car or home, or get a loan. That meant he needed money. While Rutlidge and Barnes had not admitted they were being blackmailed; it seemed a safe bet to me.

I was also able to check Felix Nolan's criminal record. I was surprised he didn't have one—but of course, that could have meant he didn't have a record under this name. A man could get himself a new name, and along with it a driver's license and credit history. And if he kept his nose clean, there wouldn't be any criminal record. If "Felix

Nolan" was a phony name, he'd managed to keep himself clean. But an autopsy and check of his fingerprints would have shown his true identity. If that was the case, the cops knew what his real name was. Yet they had only questioned me about "Felix Nolan."

I wondered if Corky Barnes or Walter Rutlidge had known him under another name.

There were still a lot of questions I could ask both them, and the police. If I did ask the police, though, Hollinger would know I was working on the case.

As far as running an investigation, there was a man I could go to for some guidance. I had met Harley Rayborn several years before when he was working on a case that took him into the music business. As it turned out, I had helped him quite a bit, and he pronounced me a natural. He convinced me to work for him, and pile up the hours I needed to punch my own ticket.

Harley was an old-time PI who didn't use a computer, still did things the old way. I learned the old ways from Harley, and the new ways on my own. But I still had never run into anyone who could run an investigation like Harley could.

I turned off the computer, called Harley and offered to buy him dinner.

HARLEY PICKED one of Nashville's newer places, the Back Alley Diner. While only open two months, the owners had 30 years' experience in the business. It was located downtown in Arcade Alley, near 4th and Broadway.

Harley was there when I arrived. I was a little shocked at his appearance. I knew he was just on either side of seventy, but he looked bad. His skin was pasty and dry. He sat alone at a table. Never a clothes horse, he was swimming in the plaid shirt and windbreaker he was wearing. I tried to keep the shock off my face as I sat down opposite him.

"Hey, Harley."

"Hey, kid! How the hell are ya? Been a few weeks, ain't it?"

"I'm good," I said. "Yeah, it's been a while."

"How's the music?"

"It's still in me," I said, tapping Clapton with my hand. It was Harley who gave me the Taylor on my 30th birthday.

"Got any gigs comin' up?"

"A few, yeah." Finally, I couldn't take it anymore. "Jesus, Harley, what's up?"

"I don't look so good, huh?" His eyes were bloodshot, and his hands were shaky.

"You look like crap."

"Yeah, well . . . cancer'll do that to ya."

"Cancer?" Now I was shocked. "When? How?"

"How, I ain't sure. When? I've known a couple of months."

"Wha—? Why didn't you tell me?"

"Because I knew you'd react like this," he said.

"Like what?"

"All emotional, and shit."

"And you're not?"

"I was, for a while, but not anymore."

"Well . . . what's going on? What are they doing for you?"

"Oh, they wanna cut it out," he said, "give me some radiation, and then chemo."

"When do you start?"

"I ain't."

"What do you mean, you ain't?"

"Kid," he said, "I'm seventy-two years old and I got colon cancer. You know what the rest of my life would be like if I let them do all that? Crappin' into a bag on my chest? Losin' my hair, tossin' my cookies every day? Jesus, that chemo stuff, it almost kills ya while it's curin' ya—and then there's no guarantee. Uh-uh, not for me."

"So what are you going to do?"

"I'm gonna live, and wait," he said. "And I'm gonna eat, drink, cuss, smoke, and fuck, if I can ever get it up again."

"Harley, you can't—"

"No!" he said, sharply. The other diners around us looked over. He smiled, waved a hand of apology, and lowered his voice. "Don't tell me what I can and cannot do, Auggie. I already decided, and I ain't changin' my mind. So let's eat, have a beer, and you tell me what's on your mind. You need help?"

"Yeah," I said, "yeah, Harley, I need help."

"Okay," Harley said, "gimme the story."

WE HAD PULLED-PORK sandwiches and cold beer. People around us were having the five-dollar martinis the place had already become known for, but we preferred beer.

Harley ate with gusto, not like a man in a hurry, but like a man who enjoyed every bite. I guess that was what facing your own mortality did for you. Made you enjoy life more.

I told him the whole story, from when I met with Barnes and Rutlidge, to when I came back and was questioned by the cops. Then I told him my most recent conversation with the Major Country Music Producer and his lawyer.

"Jesus Christ," he said, "they sure dangled the right carrot in front of your nose, didn't they?"

"Fuckin'-A," I said, "and I know it, Harley, so don't try to tell me how dumb I am—"

"Hey, not me, kid," he said, cutting me off. "I'm the last guy to tell somebody how dumb they're being, right?"

"You're not being dumb doing what's right for you, are you, Harley?"

"No, kid, you ain't."

16

"Okay," Harley said, "first you gotta realize you're pokin' around in an active murder case. The cops ain't gonna like that."

"Tell me something I don't know."

"You figure a way around it?"

"Not yet."

"Well," he said, "you get that music exec to hire you to find the attaché case."

"That's already done, Harley."

"Yeah, well, he'll have to make it crystal clear to the cops or they'll toss your ass into a cell sure as I'm sittin' on a butt load of cancer."

"Harley, do we have to—"

"It ain't gonna go away because we don't talk about it, Auggie," he said. "Better to joke than try to ignore it. 'cause believe me, this thing won't be ignored."

"Okay," I said, "what else can I do?"

"You can't actually look for the thing," Harley said, "you're gonna hafta work the murder. Look into this guy Nolan's life, his background."

"I did a computer search—"

"Fuck that!" People looked around and Harley did the "sorry" wave again. "You gotta hit the bricks, kid. This is gonna be about legwork. And I'll tell ya somethin' else."

"What?"

"That record guy, Barnes? Take a look at his life, too. Him and the lawyer. These three were workin' something crooked, and you got dragged into it."

"Not so much dragged," I said, "as sucked."

"Well," Harley said, "you can still get out, forget about the recording deal."

"Harley—"

"What about doin' it yerself?"

"Recording my own music?"

"Yeah, and sellin' 'em. Lotsa people are doin' that. Writers are publishin' their own books and puttin' them on that whatayacallit . . ."

"Kindle."

"Yeah, and you musician guys you got them computer things . . ."

"Downloads. Itunes."

"Right."

I shook my head. "I can't do that, Harley."

"Why not?"

"Because as far as I'm concerned, it's not real. I mean, anybody with some disposable income can record a CD and then sell it. That doesn't make it good."

"Yeah, but yours'll be good."

"I know that," I said, "and the other thing is once you record the CD you've pretty much got to carry a box of 'em under your arm and sell 'em. I don't have time for that."

"Well," Harley said, "it's up to you. As long as you're

tryin', those bastards are always gonna have the carrot and the stick."

"I know that, Harley."

"What about, you know," he lowered his voice, " 'the song'?"

"I don't want to talk about it."

"You still gettin' money from that?"

"I get a check now and then."

"Why don't you just go ahead and write some other songs like that one?"

"Never," I said. "Never again, Harley!"

"Okay, okay," he said, "don't get testy with a dyin' old man."

"Jeez."

"I'm just fuckin' with yer head, kid. How about another beer?"

"Sure," I said, "then I've got to get going."

AFTER I PAID THE BILL, we walked outside. He wasn't moving all that well. I wondered how much pain every step was causing him.

"Hey, kid," he said, "you know if I could, I'd work this one for ya, but I ain't takin' too many cases, these days. I'm sorta semi-retired, you know?"

"I know, Harley."

He took a deep breath, then started coughing. When he stopped, he took out a cigarette and lit it up.

"I wonder if it's this fuckin' place?" he said. "You know, the air here?"

"You mean in Nashville?"

"Yeah," he said, "maybe if I'd stayed in Chicago . . ."

"Harley, you left twenty years ago—you said you were two steps ahead of a bullet."

"Tell you the truth, kid," he said, "I'd rather die from a bullet than this shit. This is fucked up, you know?"

"Yeah," I said, "I know, Harley."

17

AFTER WE MUSTERED OUT OF THE SERVICE AND returned home from Afghanistan, I didn't go home. Terry convinced me to go back to Austin, where he grew up, instead of going back to Brooklyn, New York. There we played the clubs on 6th Street, which was to Austin what Beale Street was to Memphis, and Printers Alley was to Nashville. Still having never had formal lessons, I honed my craft, by playing with better and better musicians, until I was confident enough to sit in and jam with anyone.

After Austin we traveled around the West, playing different cities and venues until we came to a parting of the ways. Terry wanted to go back to Austin where he was comfortable. He said he hadn't developed at the same rate I had, and he didn't have the same confidence. He would only hold me back. Looking at our situation dispassionately, I had to agree. So Terry went home, and I went to Nashville . . .

I HEADED HOME, feeling worse than when I'd left. Harley

had hugged me. He was never a hugger. He'd felt like a bundle of dry sticks. It scared me, thinking about a world without Harley Rayborn.

When I got to the Bourbon the place was jumping. I didn't know who was playing, but from outside they sounded pretty good. I decided I didn't want to be alone, so I went in.

I made my way to the bar and found a seat. There were four guys up on stage I didn't recognize. The Bourbon had live blues every night of the week and served great Cajun food. You never know who's going to be on the stage when you walk in. One night I got there, and Gretchen Wilson was playing (we didn't meet that night), another night it was Lil' Brian and the Zydeco Travelers. It was a blues club, but they catered to almost every taste.

Legendary names had jammed on the Bourbon Stage. Bad Company, K.C. and the Sunshine Band, Tanya Tucker, Etta James, Johnny Lang, Greg Allman and—believe it or not—James Brown.

On this night, for all I knew, these four guys had come in separately and decided to jam. Two guys from the house band sat in the audience, enjoying the music.

I knew the bartender's name was Brian. He came over, and I mimed a bottle of beer. By the time he got back, the musicians had taken a break.

"Y'all gonna play tonight?" Brian asked as he handed me my beer.

I shook my head. "Just here to drink and listen." After my talk with Harley, I wasn't in the mood to play.

Brian nodded, went off to serve another customer.

Someone rushed up and bumped into me. It was J.P. Hobbs. All of the legends in Nashville were not musicians. Big J.P., well over sixty in my estimation, and well over six feet, was a legendary roadie. He had been on tour with Johnny Cash, Merle Haggard, Hank Williams Jr., Tammy Wynette, Conway Twitty and scores of other music city legends.

I met J.P. almost as soon as I arrived in Nashville, and we hit it off. It didn't take me long to realize that many of his stories of the road were tall tales, but I enjoyed them, anyway. And we all know there's a kernel of truth in everything. It was fun trying to figure out which stories were real, and which weren't.

"Hey, Auggie!" he exclaimed, slapping me on the back. He regarded me from beneath the brim of his straw cowboy hat. It was the same one he'd been wearing for years; otherwise, every time he bought a new one he made sure it was punctured and worn in the same places. "Why are you drinkin' hand over fist?"

"I got some bad news tonight, J.P."

"Aw, man," he said, draping an arm like a log across my shoulders, "sorry to hear that. What kind of news?"

I told him about Harley.

"The private eye guy? Man that sucks," he said. "But he can't just give up. He has to go for the treatments."

"Why? He's right about chemo. I've seen people who have been on that stuff. Sometimes what's left of their life isn't worth living."

"But at least they're still living."

"What's so great about that?" I asked. "It's the quality that's important."

"Not to a poor little Catholic guy like me," he said. "I was raised to hang onto life with both hands."

I knew J.P. lived life with both hands; I didn't know about hanging on to it.

"Not me," I said. "It has to be worth it, first. Lemme buy you a drink."

"Tequila."

Brian brought the drinks, set them down and left.

"Here's to life," he said, raising his drink.

I lifted my glass and said, "No, here's to a life worth living."

AFTER A FEW MORE DRINKS J.P. SLAPPED ME on the shoulder, squeezed and said, "You know what you need, buddy?"

"A good night's sleep?"

"Nope," J.P. said, "you need what I call a 'Nashville Night.' Let's go."

"Where?"

He got off his stool and lifted me off mine. After years of carrying drum sets, and amps—equipment that was getting larger and larger over the years—lifting me was a cinch for him.

"We're gonna do Nashville," he said, "and we're gonna start at the Bluebird."

18

THE BLUEBIRD IS A LEGEND. IT'S LOCATED IN A STRIP mall just outside of downtown Nashville. The menu includes appetizers, salads, and sandwiches, and it has a full bar. A 100-seat venue, the stage has been graced by everyone from amateurs to greats. The only rule is that all sets must be acoustic. No amps need apply.

The Bluebird has been used many times as the setting for documentaries or scenes in movies. At present, it appeared in almost every episode of the TV show *Nashville*. So at any given time, there could be a film crew in there.

Not tonight.

The Bluebird turned out to be third on our list. J.P. had intended to go right there from the Bourbon, but he was almost incapable of driving past a club without going in and having at least one drink. And telling five stories. Especially when he was having one of his "Nashville Nights," which had been known to go on for days.

By the time we entered I was drunk, while J.P.—who had been drinking two to my one—was only about two sheets to the wind. His big body seemed to have an uncanny ability to process liquor. I could count on the fingers of one hand the times I'd seen him roaring drunk. Normally, he was a happy drunk. Roaring drunk he changed and went looking for fights. That was why I tried not to go out drinking with him. Tonight, however, it seemed fitting.

We found a table for four near the bar and ordered tequila. Oh, table for four. That's right. We managed to pick up two girls in the first—or second—club, and took them with us to the Bluebird. They had been fascinated by J.P.'s stories, especially with me there to back him up.

A brunette and a redhead, they were in their thirties, a couple of tourists who were in town for a cosmetics convention. They were attractive enough but seemed to be wearing most of the items they sold in their everyday lives —eyeshadow, eyeliner, lipstick, perfume . . . they especially loved J.P.'s stories about the queens of country.

"There was that time I went all night with Tammy Wynette's hairdresser," he'd said, earlier that night. "That was at a theater in Chicago, and if you go backstage, you'll find the shiny spot that little gal's bare backside rubbed into the floor. Still there. Swear to God."

The women had looked at me and I'd only nodded. I think all they managed to hear was J.P. saying "Tammy Wynette" and "Loretta Lynn." They were missing the parts when he said "hairdresser" or "assistant."

The waitress brought our drinks—wine for the ladies, tequila for us—and we looked up at the stage, where a young man and a woman were singing a love song with the backup of a bass player and drummers. The man was strumming an acoustic guitar, while the girl had her hands folded primly in her lap. They were okay, but in the Bluebird, everybody was accorded the same respect. Even J.P.—normally a loud, happy drunk—kept silent until they were finished, and then applauded enthusiastically.

"So why do they call you J.P.?" one of the women asked.

"Hell, darlin'," he said, "that's my name."

"J.P.?" the other woman asked. "Just initials?"

"Come on, J.P.," I said. "Tell 'em."

"Tell us what?"

"Ah, it ain't' nothin'," the big man said.

"J.P.'s parents were big Beatles fans," I said. "They hated country music. And when J.P. was born, they decided to name him after two of the Beatles."

"Ringo and . . ." one of the women said, but then she got stumped and her friend wasn't any help.

"John and Paul," I said.

The two women looked at me blankly.

"John Lennon and Paul McCartney?"

J.P. took a swig from his drink. He hated this story.

"Hey," one of the girls said, "Paul McCartney and Wings, right?"

I looked at J.P. and he just shrugged.

"Auggie!"

I turned at the sound of my name and saw two guys coming at me with their arms outstretched.

"Parnell? Al?"

Parnell Collins and Al Hall were a couple of musicians I had played some sessions with when I first came to Nashville. Since then they had become a pretty successful duo. Maybe they were no danger to Brooks and Dunn—or even Hall and Oates—but they had a recording deal and had put out three albums that had cracked the Top 40. They were about my age, no facial hair—unlike the aforementioned duos—both good guitarists, songwriters and singers.

"Hey, guys." I stood up and endured two man hugs. "You guys know J.P.?"

"Yeah, from the road," Parnell said. "Hey, man."

"Hey."

"Hello, ladies," Al said.

I'd forgotten their names, so I just said, "Ladies, this is Collins, and this is Hall." They stared at me. I said, "Collins and Hall, the duo?"

"Oh," one of them said.

The other one turned to J.P.

"What are you doin' here?" Parnell asked.

"Just havin' a few drinks and listenin' to some tunes," I said.

"Hey, man," Al said, "we're goin' on next. You should come up and play."

"Yeah," Parnell said, "you got your axe with you?"

"Nope, not tonight," I said. "Tonight I'm just part of the audience. You guys go ahead and do your thing."

"Well, okay," Parnell said, "but how about a beer after?"

"That I can do," I promised.

"Collins and Hall!" somebody said from the stage.

"That's us," Al said. "Gotta run."

They went up to the stage, where several guitars were waiting for them, all acoustic, of course. There was a smattering of applause that increased when they picked up their instruments.

"Ladies and gents, thanks for havin' us at the Bluebird," Parnell said. "We love playin' this venue when we're in Nashville."

"But before we get started we want to introduce a friend of ours in the audience," Al said. "In fact, we want him to come up and play with us. He's a kick-ass guitar player and a pretty fair singer. Please help us to welcome Nashville's own Auggie Velez!"

They weren't the types to take no for an answer.

"Come on!" Parnell said, not to me but the crowd, and they started to applaud.

"You better get up there, boy," J.P. said.

"Yeah," I said. I didn't feel like performing, but now there were too many people to turn down. I got up, made my way to the stage while people reached out to slap me on the back and the arms.

"You guys . . ." I said as I stepped up on stage.

"Pick out an axe, bud," Parnell said. "Just a couple songs, okay?"

"Sure," I said, picking up an Epiphone Acoustic that was too expensive for me to own.

"We think you'll know this one," Al said to me.

They started playing and I seamlessly blended in with them. After all, it was one of my songs.

19

I DID THREE SONGS WITH THEM—ONE OF MINE, TWO OF theirs—and then got off the stage to some pretty good applause. I rejoined J.P. and the girls. He slapped me hard enough on the back to dislodge a molar and they smiled and applauded.

They finished up their set and I excused myself to meet them at the bar for a couple of drinks. We exchanged news items and life stories since we hadn't seen each other in some months, and then they had to leave. I went back to J.P. and his ladies.

"Excuses us," one of the women said, "we need to go and powder our noses."

It seemed to me they were wearing plenty of powder, but J.P. smiled, doffed his hat and said, "Hurry back, ladies."

They smiled and hurried off.

"Which one you want, son?"

"You can have 'em both, J.P.," I said. "After these drinks, I'm headin' home."

"Hell, son, you can't do that," he said. "We're almost ready to close the deal."

"I'm not in the mood to play, J.P.," I said. "And while I appreciate the sentiment, I'm not ready for one of your marathon Nashville Nights."

"Auggie—" He grabbed my arm.

"What?"

Suddenly, J.P. looked distressed.

"What's wrong, J.P.?" I'd already had enough bad news about a friend that night. I hoped there wasn't more coming.

"You know of anybody goin' out on the road?" he asked. "Maybe they need an experienced roadie?"

"Um, well, there's always somebody goin' out," I said. "I could check—"

"Couldja?" He tightened his grip on my arm. "That'd be good, son, real good." He released his grip and patted me on the shoulder.

I suddenly realized it wasn't me who needed this night of bar-hopping, but J.P. I realized that he hadn't once told any stories of a recent tour he'd been on. All his stories were about tours in the past.

"Just don't make it anythin' with that Taylor Swift chick," he said quickly, as the ladies appeared and started across the room. "I still got *some* pride left."

EVEN AT HIS AGE, J.P. was still a charmer. His county boy exterior had always attracted women, and if these two ladies were any indication, he still had it. They were both paying rapt attention to him and his stories, and I wondered what their conversation in the ladies room had been like.

"You can have the young one."

"No, that's okay, you can have the young one."

Well, many of J.P.'s stories included nights with two or more women, and some of those had to be true. For that reason, I knew he'd be fine if I left him there with these nice ladies.

"So this time," he was saying as I started to stand, "I was with Dolly Parton's wardrobe girl . . . where you goin', Auggie?"

"I gotta go, J.P.," I said. "Ladies, it was a pleasure."

They both nodded at me, probably glad I was leaving.

"Auggie," J.P. said, extending his arm toward me, "you'll call me, right?"

"As soon as I know something, J.P.," I promised.

I was weaving towards the door when I heard one of the women ask him, "Have you ever been on tour with Taylor Swift?"

I don't remember much after that.

20

WHEN I WOKE UP THE NEXT MORNING, I FELT A WARM hip pressed against mine. Before I turned over, I tried to remember what had happened the night before so that I wouldn't be surprised. I recalled my conversation with Harley, drinking at the Bourbon, and J.P. showing up. Nothing in my fuzzy brain about a girl—just two women I thought I had left with J.P. I rolled over slowly and looked, hoping against hope it wasn't J.P.

(One time, years ago, we were on the road; five of us were sharing a room in a hotel. I was bushed and crashed before Elton arrived. The phone rang and woke me up; it was Elton. "Will you tell this broad behind the desk to gimme a key and the room number? She won't let me up." He put the girl on the phone and I told her to let him come up. He burst into the room announced that he was exhausted, looked around, didn't see an available bed or rollaway, promptly stripped down to his underwear—not a pretty sight, because Elton is all bones and ribs—and got into bed with me. I heard about that for years.)

Not J.P.

I had obviously picked up somebody at the bar and brought her upstairs with me. I tried to remember her. She was my type—right age (late 20's), slender, auburn hair and pretty, even with her face scrubbed of make-up (always a plus). But one-night stands were not my style. I didn't like them on the road, and no better at home. So I was uncomfortable.

I eased out of bed without waking her, picked up my boxer shorts from the floor. Unlike the rest of the loft, my bathroom was enclosed, so I was able to close the door and take a shower without waking her.

Wearing the same boxer shorts, I made coffee. The smell probably woke her. I heard her stir and poured two cups, carried one to the bed.

She sat up, stretched interestingly, then put her hands down on the bed and stared at me with a big smile.

"Oh my," she said. "Good-mornin'."

"Morning. Coffee?"

"Thanks."

She reached for the cup, totally unconcerned by the fact that she was naked. She had tits like ripe peaches, with big pink nipples. I dragged my eyes away from them and looked at her face. It was then I recognized her.

"Jesus," I said, "Allegra?"

She smiled. "You remember."

"Not much," I admitted. "How—why—"

"You called me," she said. "Said you were at this bar and would I come and meet you. You needed a ride."

"And you agreed?"

"The other day, in Mr. Barnes's office, I thought y'all were cute. I kinda thought you'd call me—and for a different reason."

I was starting to remember. When I got outside the

Bluebird, I realized I had gone there in J.P.'s truck. I was drunk—too drunk to even wander the streets trying to find a cab. And if I went back inside and had them call me a cab, I thought I might end up getting rolled.

I went through my pockets and came with the piece of paper with Allegra's number on it. I guess I called her. . . .

"Do you have something I could wear?" Allegra asked.

"Oh, sure," I said. I thought about grabbing the Clapton shirt from the foot of the bed and tossing it to her, but instead, I opened the top drawer of my dresser. There was a collection of T-shirts there, but the one I took out was one that had been given to me as a gift. It was too small for me—the smallest I owned—and I tossed it to her.

"When I got there," Allegra said, pulling the Nancy Wilson shirt over her head—shifting the cup from one hand to the other. "You'd had a few drinks already. We went to a small bar down the streets. You bought me a few, we talked—"

"About what?"

"Well, you *told* me you wanted to talk about what happened in Mr. Barnes's office, and why I got transferred, but we got sidetracked and then came up here and . . . got sidetracked in a different way." She batted her lashes at me to make her point.

"Oh . . . I remember . . ."

"I'm flattered you remember," she said.

She got out of bed and walked around. The T-shirt almost covered her pubic bush, but she seemed comfortable enough. She went to the window and stood there, looking out and sipping. From behind, I could see the smooth cheeks of her neat ass.

"It's sure is pretty here," she said.

"Yes, it is."

"You told me last night how you got this place temporarily and couldn't leave. In the daylight, I can truly see why."

I took my coffee over to stand next to her and look out.

"Is that music I hear?" she asked.

"Always," I said. "It seems to float on the air. That's one of the things that's kinda cool about living here."

"Well," she said, "this *is* Nashville."

"Allegra," I said, "would you mind talking about—I mean, I don't really remember—"

"I'll talk about whatever you want," she said, batting her pretty eyes at me, "if you buy me breakfast."

"Deal," I said.

21

HARLEY SAID NOT TO LOOK FOR THE ATTACHÉ CASE, BUT to look at Felix Nolan's life. That meant going to Nolan's home, in Germantown.

GERMANTOWN WAS NORTH NASHVILLE. It enjoyed the title of Nashville's first subdivision. It eventually fell into disrepair and many of the buildings were scheduled for demolition. But as is often the case, a developer swooped in during the '70s and saved the day. Now it's a thriving urban neighborhood.

There are quite a few restaurants in Germantown, but most of them don't serve breakfast. The Drinkhaus might sound like a brewery, but in reality, it is a breakfast and lunch café.

Allegra put the same clothes back on from the night before, but by the time she came out of the bathroom, you couldn't tell. She'd done her hair and makeup and looked fresh for the day. She'd worn a tight, scoop-necked top and jeans to the bar, and the clothes fit the Drinkhaus, as well.

I had my Jimmy Page shirt showing him wielding his Gibson Les Paul Classic.

We ordered and faced each other over coffee.

"How can I help you, Auggie?" Allegra asked.

"When I was up in your boss's office he hired me to do a job. I had to deliver something to a man. Now that man's been killed, and I need to prove to the police that I only met him once, and that was because Corky was paying me."

"So you want me to tell them you were up there?"

"Yes."

"And that you were paid?"

"Yes."

She hesitated, then asked, "Would I have to do this in court? Under oath?"

"No," I said. "The detectives will probably just ask you some questions—if they haven't already."

"Oh, no," she said, "I haven't spoken to any police detectives."

"Okay, then," I said. "They'll probably be stopping by to see you soon."

The waitress came with our breakfasts and set them down. We started to eat.

"Auggie," she said, "I can tell them that I saw you in the office, but . . ."

"But what?" I asked. "It's okay, Allegra. Say what you have to say."

"Well . . . I don't know that Mr. Barnes paid you anything," she said.

"Don't you see any papers or files when he makes a payment?"

"If he cut a check, but not if he paid you in cash. Did he?"

"Yeah," I said, "yeah, he paid me in cash."

"Then you can't prove you were paid."

"No," I said, "not unless he or Rutlidge admit it."

"And why won't they?"

"I don't know," I said. "Something's hinky about the whole thing."

"Can't you show the police you deposited in your bank?" she asked.

"They already know that," I said, "but it could be because the dead guy paid me for . . . something."

"What do you they think—" She stopped and her eyes went wide. "That you were selling drugs?"

"I don't *know* what they think," I said. "But I'm afraid that's it."

"And Mr. Barnes won't tell the truth?"

"Not yet," I said, "maybe not ever."

"So, what are you going to do?"

"I'm going to try to clear myself," I said.

"How do you know how to do that?"

"I'm a private detective," I said.

She frowned. "I thought you were a musician."

"I do the detective stuff on the side. I guess I didn't tell you that last night?"

"Oh," she said, "so that's why Mr. Barnes hired you. He needed a detective. That's kinda cool."

"You had no idea why I was up there, did you?" I asked.

"No." She shrugged. "I'm sorry I won't be much help to you."

I guess I didn't want to believe that, at the moment, so I decided to tell her more.

"Does the name Felix Nolan mean anything to you?"

She thought a moment, chewing on some bacon, then said, "No, huh-uh. Should it?"

"Well, Corky was apparently doing some business with him."

"He's the dead guy?"

"Yeah."

"Mr. Barnes does a lot of business with a lot of people," she said, "and I wasn't privy to all of it."

"You mean he made some . . . shady deals?"

"I can't say they were shady, exactly," she said, "but I suppose there's a lot of . . . stuff that goes on at that level, you know?"

"And some of it they wouldn't let you in on."

"They had lots of late nights there, Auggie, after they sent me home."

"Corky, Rutlidge . . . and who else?"

"I don't know," she said. "I think the two of them are the only ones who know everything that goes on at Starcade."

"But if there was another person who would know, who would it be?"

"I guess, maybe . . . Andy Pac?" She spelled it.

"Who is Pac?"

"Head of A&R? He's worked up there for a long time. Except for Mr. Rutlidge and Mr. Barnes, he knows more about what's going on than anyone."

"Andy Pac," I repeated. "What's he look like?" She gave me a quick description. "Okay. Maybe you have helped me, after all."

"How?"

"You gave me a name I didn't have before."

She wiped her mouth with a napkin, smiled and asked, "Does that mean y'all will call me again?"

"Could be."

. . .

AT THE END OF BREAKFAST, she asked, "What are you going to do now?"

"Felix Nolan lived near here. I'm gonna go over and take a look around."

"Private eye work!" she said. "Can I come?"

"Don't you have to go to work?"

"Not really,' she said. "When Mr. Barnes told you I was reassigned?"

"Yes."

"What he meant was, he fired me."

"Fired? But why?"

"Well, either I wasn't doing my job right," she said, "or I saw or heard something I wasn't supposed to."

"That night? The night I was there?"

She shrugged. "Anyway, I don't have anything else to do, so . . ."

She stood there expectantly; I guess waiting to be asked along. But I really didn't need a partner. I also didn't need anyone along to see what a bumbler I might turn out to be at "private eye work."

"I can't take you, Allegra," I said. "I don't know what I might have to do while I'm there."

"You mean you might have to do something . . ." she lowered her voice, ". . . illegal?"

"Maybe, who knows?"

She leaped in place and said, "I could be your lookout!"

"Allegra—"

"All right, all right," she said, "maybe we can do break-ing-and-entering on our second date?"

"Has this been a date?" I asked.

"Well . . . it's the morning after, isn't it?" she asked.

"It is definitely the morning after," I said.

"Then I'll go home, and sit by the phone and wait for your call for our second date."

"Don't you have to look for a new job?"

"You haven't done that in a while, have you?" she asked. "I can do that from home, on the web, and submit resumes the same way."

"Okay," I said, "so you go home and do that, and I'll do my job."

"What about your other job?" she asked. "When do I get to hear some of your music?"

"That," I said, "sounds like third date territory."

22

Felix Nolan's Germantown home was a brick building with eight apartments, each apartment with its own entrance off an open-sided breezeway. That was good. I didn't have to go through a hallway. I still might run into another tenant, but I wouldn't have to explain how I got inside.

The apartments had letters on the doors. Nolan's was on the second floor, apartment G. Standing in front of his door, across from apartment F, I couldn't hear any sounds in the building. Maybe I got lucky. Everyone else might have gone to work.

I tried the doorknob, wasn't surprised to find it locked. That would've been too easy. The bad part about the way the apartments were set up was that I had no access to windows.

Sometimes, when in the office with Harley, he'd tell me stories about "the old days." During one of those stories, he made a gift to me of a set of lockpicks. After that, we spent a lot of hours getting me acquainted with them. Not particularly proficient, but acquainted.

Harley had heard me play guitar and one day he asked, "How can someone with your nimble fingers be so bad at this?"

I was about to find out how bad I was because I had never tried to use them for real, before.

I took the little leather case out of my pocket and unzipped it. After a walk to the stairway to make sure no one was around, I knelt before the door and inserted the picks. Despite what you might have seen on television a lock cannot be picked one-handed with one tool. A nail file or hairpin just doesn't do the job. It takes a torsion wrench and a pick. The wrench is used to apply torque and hold the pins in place once they're picked. While it's called "picking a lock" there is more than one pick to maneuver. Once they've all been "picked" the torsion wrench is also turned, used as a key to open the lock.

This is extremely sensitive work. If you drop the picked pins, you have to start over. Harley could have done the job in under a minute. It took me seven; although I could have sworn I was at it for half an hour. Sweating, every sound I heard convinced me I was about to be caught. Finally, I got the final pin in place and turned the lock. The door opened. I stepped inside quickly, shut the door and pressed my back to it. Thankfully, the air-conditioner had been left on. I stood there for several minutes, cooling off.

I put my tools in the leather case and back into my pocket. After a few deep breaths, I walked away from the door and into the apartment.

Most of my PI experience may have been serving papers, tailing people or stake-outs, but spending time with Harley, learning from him, was more experience than most people ever got.

He taught me how to search a room. Start with the chests and dressers, always with the bottom drawers first, leaving them open. That way you don't have to waste time closing one drawer so you can look in another. This also saves time, but it's something you can do only if you don't care that anyone knows you were there.

I decided to close the drawers afterward. The police detectives had probably been there, and they might come back. If they knew somebody had searched the apartment, they might decide to blame me.

I did as neat a search as possible. Open and close the drawers, put everything back where it was in the kitchen —that also meant leaving no sugar on the counter when I probed the bowl—replace cushions on the sofa.

In the beginning, I was looking for something the size of an attaché case. That meant looking in closets and cupboards. But when I hadn't found anything I started looking for smaller, flatter things that could fit into such a case.

I knew that Nolan had been a musician. In one closet I found—in their proper cases—a saxophone, a clarinet, and a flute. I looked beneath the instruments to see if he'd hidden anything there. I even looked inside the saxophone. The instruments were used, but they were well cared for.

I started to look through papers — bills, letters, bank statements. That's when I discovered that Felix Nolan had several bank accounts and at least one safety deposit box. The desk drawers were a mess, which led me to believe they had already been gone through—probably by the police, but what if I wasn't the first person Rutlidge and Corky had hired to look for their item?

I found a bill for a storage unit. Maybe he'd hidden

whatever I was looking for there. I folded the bill and put it in my pocket.

I closed the desk drawers. There was no safety deposit key. My bet was the cops had been there before me and taken it. They wouldn't have left the place clean and neat, the way I'd found it, however. Among the bills, I found receipts for a maid service. They had probably come in and cleaned up after the police were there. The only other explanation would have been neat police, and I wouldn't have put money on that one.

A door slammed somewhere in the building. I waited, then heard muffled music. Someone had come home, turned on the radio or CD player. From the beat, I assumed it was rap

In Nashville?

I tried to block it out and——as they say on Google— started an Advanced Search.

23

HARLEY ALWAYS TOLD ME THAT COPS THINK THEY'RE being thorough, but they can't help thinking like cops. When you're searching a home, you have to think like its occupant. If the man's an ad executive, think like an executive. If he's a mechanic, think like a mechanic. And if he's a musician . . .

I had already looked in Nolan's saxophone because that was the only instrument that seemed to have an opening large enough to hide something in. That left the clarinet and flute.

I went back to the closet and took out all three instrument cases, carried them to the living room and set them down on the floor. One by one I removed the instruments and searched them thoroughly. There wasn't much room in the flute to hide anything larger than a pebble. I removed the clarinet's mouthpiece, and saxophone's mouthpiece and still found nothing.

I set all the instruments aside on the sofa and began to search the cases. In the clarinet case, when I pulled back the lining, I found a book. A flat notebook with a blue cover, it had about fifty lined pages in it but was still flat enough to hide beneath the lining. I opened it, found some names, and numbers—long numbers, with dashes. No addresses, no phone numbers.

I put the notebook in my pocket. I didn't think it was what had been in the attaché case. It was too small. There'd be no reason to put something that small in something that large.

I pressed the lining back—it had been held in place by Velcro—then replaced the instruments in their cases and put them back in the closet.

I searched further but couldn't find anything else interesting. After that I tidied the place up, hoping nobody but a maid would be able to tell that someone went through the place.

The rap music was still playing, but as I put my hand on the door to open it, the music stopped. I stopped. Maybe the person was getting ready to leave again, and I had no idea if they were on the first floor or the second. I didn't want to run into anyone in the breezeway.

I had lived in apartment buildings before. Tenants rarely entered or left without slamming the door. It was either their way of making sure the door locked, or they did it out of total thoughtlessness toward the other tenants. I always voted for the latter.

I waited, listening for an opening or closing door. Nothing. Maybe the person had simply gotten tired of their own music.

I cracked the door, looked outside, didn't see anybody, so I stepped outside quickly and pulled the door shut behind me. At that moment the door to apartment F opened and a woman stepped out. She stopped short when she saw me, looking surprised.

"Can I help you?" she asked, looking me up and down frankly.

"Yeah," I said, pointing at the G in Nolan's door, "I was looking for Felix?"

"Are you a friend of his?" she asked.

"No, not really."

"Are you lookin' to cause him some trouble?"

She was an attractive enough woman in her forties who was probably a looker ten years ago. Her Southern accent was musical, helped to still make her attractive. I had a feeling she'd like it if I was trying to cause Felix Nolan some trouble.

"I might be," I said. "Why?"

She shrugged. "Seems to me somebody was always comin' around to cause that boy trouble."

"Anybody in particular?"

"Just some men," she said, "different men."

"Were you friends with Felix?"

She laughed. "You don't have to be friends to fuck somebody once or twice, honey."

I grinned back at her. "I guess that depends on whether it was once or twice."

"Come to think of it," she said, "it might've been three times."

"He's dead, you know," I said, wanting to see her reaction.

"I know," she said. "The police were around. You police?"

"What do you think?"

"Well," she said, "with that bandana on your head and the calluses on your fingers I'd say you were a musician. Guitar, right?"

"You got me."

"You play with Felix?"

"I never knew Felix really," I said. "He just . . . had something of mine. I was hoping to get in and find it."

"My name's Melanie."

"Hi, Melanie," I said, "mine's Auggie."

We shook hands. She held mine for a few extra beats before letting go.

"You wanna come in for some . . . coffee?" she asked. Or somethin'?"

"Looks to me like you were on your way out."

"Just gonna run a few errands," she said. "Nothin' important. I make a mean cup of coffee. And I like musicians." She gave me an expectant look, staring up at me. She still had pretty eyes, even if there were some lines around them.

I made a bet with myself that she had liked a lot of musicians in her time.

"I've got some business to take care of," I said. "Maybe another time."

"Yeah," she said, "sure, another time." Despite her words, she didn't seem to take the refusal personally.

She turned and headed for the stairway.

"Hey!"

"What?" she asked.

"What kind of music you like?"

"Me?" she said. "I like all kinds. But lately, I'm kinda partial to rap."

"That ain't music," I said.

She laughed and went down the stairs.

24

WHEN I GOT TO THE STREET, I TOOK OUT MY CELL phone. I used it sparingly because I didn't like it. I kept it on me in case I got a call about a gig, but other than Elton, Harley and a couple of other friends, few people had the number. I had two numbers programmed on my speed dial: Elton was 1, and Harley was 2. I pressed 2, but after ten rings there was no answer, not even his machine. That worried me. I just wanted to ask him a couple of questions about what I should do next, but when I couldn't get him, I decided to go over to his office.

SOUTH NASHVILLE COMBINES historical charm with a more modern area that appeals to businesses. Harley's office and house had been there for years, and he always refused to move downtown, even if it meant more clients.

His house was on a small street off of Murfreesboro Pike, around the corner from the renovated Altamonte Apartments. I drove there, parked right in front. Most of the houses on the street were old but had been renovated.

Harley's was the one that looked like it had fallen on hard times. I hadn't been there in a while, and I was kind of shocked at the appearance. The lawn was overgrown with weeds; shingles were hanging by a thread, the front storm door screen was torn through.

I rang the bell, got no answer. Next to the door was a small plaque that said: Harley Rayborn, Private Investigations.

"Harley?"

I went to the driveway alongside the house. Harley's Mustang was there. He'd kept the thing running by working on it himself. I didn't know if his cancer was allowing him to still do that, but the car looked okay. The fact that it was there meant he had to be inside. The way he'd been walking when I saw him just the night before showed me he probably hadn't gone for a walk.

I went back to the front door, opened the torn screen door and pounded.

"Harley! Come on, man!"

Still no answer. The door was solid, no windows. I thought about trying to find a window to look in, but finally just stepped back and kicked in the door. It took one shot. Good door, bad lock.

I rushed in and found him on the floor in the living room. He was unconscious, but there was a pulse. He didn't look like he'd been attacked, so I had to assume this was a result of his illness.

"Harley? Can you hear me?" I shook him. He moaned but didn't come around. I took out my cell and dialed 9-1-1.

THE AMBULANCE TOOK him to the emergency room at

Southern Hills Medical Center, taking Nolansville Road to Wallace Road. They pulled into Emergency and I found a place to park and ran inside.

I checked in at the desk to see where they had taken Harley and was given the runaround.

"Look," I said, "I made the call for the ambulance, I followed it here."

"Are you family, sir?"

"I'm all the family he's got," I said, truthfully.

"Just a minute," she said, "I'll have a doctor come out and speak with you."

I looked around, saw other people sitting, either waiting to be seen or for someone already inside. I didn't sit, just stood there at the desk and waited.

Eventually, a slightly harried looking young doctor came out to address me.

"Are you here with Mr. Rayborn—"

"Doc, he's got cancer. I'm not sure what kind, but—"

"Colon," the doctor said, cutting me off. "We ran him through the computer. He's actually being treated here at the cancer center. We've put in a call to his own doctor."

"How is he—"

"We're working on stabilizing him," the doctor said. His name tag said THAKCERY. I had a feeling someone had transposed the "C" and "K" in his name.

"Can I see him?"

"Not yet, sir," Dr. Thakcery said. "I understand y'all are family?"

I hesitated, then said, "Yes. My name's Auggie Velez. He's my . . . my family."

"Well, I'll let you know when we know something, or when his doctor gets here. Meanwhile, maybe there are some other calls you got to make?"

"Yeah," I said, "maybe."

And maybe not. Harley did have some family, but they lived in Chicago. A son and daughter, but I'd never had any contact with them and he hadn't seen or heard from them in years.

"I'll be around," I said.

"You get yourself some coffee," he said and went back inside.

I got myself a coffee from a vending machine and had a seat. I had nobody to call. Elton had met Harley a few times, but there was no need to call him about this.

I took out the papers I had taken from Nolan's apartment: a bank statement, the notebook, and a storage bill. I'd never get into the safe deposit box without a key, and I didn't like my chances of getting into his storage unit without a key. I wondered if the cops had been through it already. As for the book, I was thinking it was in some type of code.

I checked the address of the storage facility, saw that it was on Adams Street in East Germantown. That made sense since Nolan lived in Germantown. The location sounded familiar to me, but I couldn't place it at that moment.

My next move should probably be to drive out there and take a look, but that was going to have to wait. My primary concern at that moment was Harley. I put the papers away in my pocket and settled down to wait, like everyone else.

25

AFTER ABOUT AN HOUR ANOTHER DOCTOR CAME OUT. This one appeared to be older and calmer. He looked around, spotted me and seemed to decide I was the one to talk to.

"Are you Auggie?" he asked, approaching me.

I stood up. "That's right."

He shook my hand. "Harley's all right, for the moment. I've put him in a room." His Southern accent was barely there. Maybe he'd trained it out of himself through the years.

"What's wrong with him? Is it his cancer?"

"His cancer is kicking his ass, is what's wrong with him," he said, "and I can't get him to do anything about it. Talkin' to that man is like talkin' to a gnat on a pig's ass. Maybe y'all can talk some sense into him." As he got worked up, his accent thickened.

"Does he have a chance?" I asked. "I mean, with treatment?"

"Treatment, surgery, and treatment again could prolong his life."

"For how long?"

He looked startled. "Does that matter?"

"It does to him," I said, "but probably not as much as the quality of life you'd be giving him."

The doctor frowned. "He's already talked to you about all this. I hear his words coming back at me."

"Well, it is his decision, isn't it?" I asked. "And what about the expense of all this?"

"Don't concern yourself with that," he said. "Arrangements have been made to cover the expense."

"What kind of arrangements?"

"It would be up to him to tell you that. Look, I see the possibility of extending his life. That's my job. Y'all can talk to him about it or not. That's your business. Here's my card if you want to talk to me further."

I took the card, looked at it. Dr. Gerald Messenger, M.D. Underneath that it said: Oncology. Address on Pierce Avenue.

"Can I see him?"

"I'll walk you up."

He took me to an elevator, rode up with me and walked me to Harley's room, all without further comment. I had a distinct feeling he was unhappy with me.

I ENTERED THE ROOM, which was private. Whoever was footing the bills for Harley was getting him the best. I didn't know what that was about, but it wasn't the time to ask.

I approached the bed. Harley looked shrunken beneath the covers, his face almost skeletal. But he was breathing without the aid of any machines, although there was an intravenous drip set up.

I pulled a chair over and got comfortable, determined to sit there as long as they'd let me, or until Harley woke up and spoke to me.

It turned out both of those happened at about the same time. . . .

HARLEY'S EYES opened some time later, blinked a few times, then looked over at me.

"Hey, kid."

"How you doing, Harley?"

He frowned, said, "Okay, now."

"What happened?"

"Last thing I remember was a hot poker in my innards," Harley said. "I was tryin' for the phone, but I guess I didn't make it. How'd I get here?"

"I came by and found you on the floor. I'm afraid I kicked in your door."

"Glad you did, I guess," he said, "although, it might've been better for me and you if I'd died there on the floor."

"I talked to your doctor," I said. "Seems he doesn't like that kind of talk."

"Messenger?" he said. "Yeah, he's kind of a stickler for savin' lives."

I was about to say something when a nurse walked in and said, "Time to go, sir. Visiting hours begin again in a few hours."

I nodded to her, looked at Harley, whose eyes were at half-mast.

"I'll be back later, Harley," I said, putting my hand on his shoulder.

"I'll be here, I guess," he mumbled. "These folks'll do their damnedest to keep me alive."

"That's our job," the nurse said, with a benign smile.

He grabbed my hand then and said weakly, "Bring me a hotdog."

"Later, Harley," I said, but he had already fallen asleep.

26

TO THE COUNTRY AT LARGE—MAYBE THE WORLD—
Nashville was Music City, and that meant country. But the
truth was, Nashville was the home to all kinds of music.
When I reached the Store-It Storage Facility, I realized
why the address had sounded so familiar. It was right
across the street from the Nashville Jazz Workshop. I had
been there once or twice for a show. They also provided
lessons given by jazz professionals who donated their time.

I parked in front a gate that had an electronic lock.
Everyone who had a unit inside was given a number code
to punch into a keypad that opened the gate. Since Nolan
had a book with a bunch of numbers in it, maybe his code
was in there, too.

Of course, even if I was to get past the gate, I'd still
have to get into the unit. If it had a padlock with a key, I'd
be able to pick it, but if it had a combination lock on it, I'd
be back where I started.

I checked my watch. I had time to get something to
eat and return to the hospital for the evening visiting
hours.

. . .

A LOT of people think that the best hotdog in Nashville comes from a place called Hot Diggity Dog, but not Harley. Hot Diggity specializes in Chicago hotdogs. In fact, they say they import them from the Windy City. Harley is from New York and does not appreciate the Chicago hot dog.

I stopped in Germantown at a place called Zackie's Original Hot Dog. While they do serve Chicago style hot dogs on their menu, their dogs are Nathan's.

I sat at one of the inside stools rather than one of the two outside tables, ate a couple of dogs and fries, then bought one for Harley. I had them wrap it in aluminum foil because I had to hide not only the dog itself but the smell. They were closing as I left.

I drove to the hospital, put the dog in my back pocket with my Jimmy Page (Gibson guitar) T-shirt covering it.

As I walked into Harley's room, I noticed that he was awake. There was a nurse there, the one who had chucked me out earlier. She plumped his pillows, then turned and looked at me. I had the feeling she could tell I had the hotdog in my pocket.

"You call me if you need me, Mr. Rayborn," she said, and left, giving me one last look.

I approached the bed.

"You got my hotdog?" he asked, immediately.

I took it from my pocket and handed it to him.

"Zackie's?"

"Where else?"

"I'm glad you didn't hide it in your pants."

"I might have impressed your nurse that way."

He stuck it under his pillow. "I'll eat it later. That

woman made me eat a meatloaf that tasted like a damned dirty sponge and some watery vegetables. Stood there and watched me eat it. She likes me."

"Guess that's why she was looking at me so hard."

"You talk to my doctor?"

"I did."

"When am I gettin' outta here?"

"I'm not sure, Harley. He didn't say. He doesn't like me much. By the way, I told everybody I was family."

"You are, kid," he said. "My only family. Thought you knew that."

"Harley," I said, "maybe these folks know what they're talking about—"

"Auggie, I've talked to people who've had chemo," Harley said. "It knocks the crap outta them. They can't eat. I love my hotdogs, Auggie. If I couldn't eat 'em? I wouldn't wanna live."

"Okay, Harley," I said. "I'm sure your doctor'll come and see you."

"That guy!" Harley said. "My regular guy sent me to him. He's got a bad attitude."

"He said something about the expenses being taken care of?"

"Oh, that," Harley said. "I got an old client still feels like she owes me. When she found out I was sick, she insisted on taking care of the bills."

"Is that why you don't want treatments?" I asked. "You don't want her to have to pay the bills?"

"Hell, no!" he said. "If I wanted the damn treatments I'd let 'er go ahead and pay for 'em. Read my lips, kid. I don't want any of it! Chemo, radiation, rippin' out my asshole? None of it!"

"Okay," I said, "calm down. Your nurse'll come in and give me hell."

"Pull up a chair and tell me about your case. What'd you do today?"

I ran it down for him.

"Sounds like you did a good search," he said. "How long did the lock take you?"

"Um, about . . . four minutes," I lied.

"More than that, I bet," he said, "but you just need more practice. So, do you think you can figure out his code?"

"I don't know," I said. "I might need somebody who's better with numbers than I am."

"Well, that ain't me. I know lots of people, but no code breakers. How you gonna get into the storage unit?"

"I don't know."

"And the bank?"

"I don't think I can get into the bank."

"Well, the storage unit, then. And what about this other guy?"

"Which guy?"

"The guy the secretary told you about. Pac?"

"Yeah, Andy Pac."

"You talk to him, yet?"

"No."

"You gotta do that. Get him alone and see how much he knows."

"Yeah, okay," I said.

"Can you pick him out? She tell you what he looks like?"

"Yeah, he should be easy to spot," I said. "He's Asian."

"That's good," he said. "The Chinks are sneaky. He'll know stuff. I bet he'll know a lot."

To say Harley wasn't politically correct was an understatement.

"I'll find out."

Harley winced and said, "Damn."

"You okay?"

"Just some pain. Where's that damn button?"

"Here." It was a handheld button on a cord. He pressed it.

"I'll let you get some rest," I said. "You got my cell. If you're getting out tomorrow, call me and I'll pick you up."

"Okay," he said. "After Nursie leaves me alone I'm gonna have my hotdog. Thanks."

"I'll see you soon, Harley."

He grabbed my arm.

"Go back to my house, get my phone book, and call Chummy. You don't know him, but he can help you with the storage unit."

"Okay, Harley."

"And keep the book," he said. "It's yours now." He got a faraway look in his eyes and released my arm.

I passed the nurse on the way out and she gave me another hard look.

"How you doin', Sweetie . . ." I heard her say as she entered the room.

27

ANDY PAC WOULD HAVE TO WAIT UNTIL TOMORROW, Wednesday. If I didn't catch him at work, I'd have to wait another day or track him down at home.

I got in my car and drove back to Harley's house. The front door was wide open. I went to his desk and found his phone book. It was a leather bound, large planner. It had all the numbers of contacts he used in his business and was important to him.

I found a hammer and some nails and nailed the front door shut. Then I went out the back door, locking it behind me.

Since getting back from the tour I hadn't had time to shop for groceries, so I stopped in a small supermarket and picked up some fruit. I love fruit, usually keep a couple of bowls of it around. I bought green grapes, plums, peaches, bananas, and apples. I also bought a small container of cut up pineapple.

From there I drove home. I intended to leaf through Harley's book for Chummy, a name I'd never heard before. I put my car in the parking lot I used and walked to my building. It didn't surprise me to see Hollinger and Lewis waiting in front of my door. I figured they'd want to see me every day, so I wouldn't get too complacent. I had a plastic bag of groceries in each hand and Harley's phone book under my arm.

"There's our boy," Hollinger said.

Lewis turned, looked at me with his arms folded. "Looks like he's been doin' some shoppin'."

"Didn't we just talk yesterday?" I asked.

"That's the thing about an investigation," Hollinger said. "There's always new questions popping up. Where you been, Auggie?"

"Is that one of the new questions that popped up?"

"No, Rockford," Lewis said. "Save the clever remarks."

"You guys want to come upstairs?" I asked.

"Not really," Lewis said. "We just have a few questions."

"What are you reading, Auggie?"

"It's my day planner."

"You got your day planned? We holdin' you up?" Lewis asked.

"No," I said. "I had an appointment this afternoon. Now I just want to go upstairs, relax and have a beer."

"You mean you ain't been workin' the case today?" Lewis asked.

"What case? Oh, you mean your case? Did you want my help with that?"

"Every PI thinks they're clever, right?" Lewis asked his partner.

"If we need help, kid, we won't ask an amateur."

"Fine," I said. "Call me an amateur if it makes you feel better about yourselves. What questions did you have for me?"

Hollinger looked at Lewis.

"What did you want to ask him?"

"Me?" Lewis said. "I thought you had a question for him."

"Your Penn and Teller sucks," I said, then looked at Lewis. "You talk too much."

"Hey," Lewis said, "that one actually wasn't bad."

"I guess we have no questions for you, after all," Hollinger said. "But if we do think of any, we'll be in touch."

"So this was just harassment?"

"Naw," Lewis said, "just a mistake."

"A mistake?"

"Everybody makes 'em," Hollinger said.

Lewis stopped to look into my bags, then reached in and plucked out an apple.

"Thanks," he said, cleaning it on his arm and then taking a bite.

I wanted to say, "Choke on it," but instead I said, "You're welcome."

They walked away. Were they just trying to shake me up, or keep me off balance?

I went up the stairs and stopped in front of my door. Had they been inside? Searching? Maybe planting some bugs?

I put both grocery bags in my left hand, still balancing the phone book under my arm, then unlocked the door and went inside. I put the grocery bags down on the kitchen counter, and the phone book on the table.

Walking around, I looked for anything out of place that would indicate a search. Harley had not only taught me to do a neat search but to detect one, as well.

But I didn't see anything. Last thing I did was check my guitars. Hollinger had demonstrated an interest in them and might have had to touch them if he was inside. Each one was in its place, though. Even the few that were stored in cases.

As far as I could tell, the cops had not been in my place. They'd just been waiting out front to . . . to what?

I went back to the kitchen to wash my fruit and lay it out in a couple of bowls. Then I poured some Rice Krispies into a bowl, added grapes and milk and ate it as my dinner while looking out the window.

28

THE NEXT MORNING I REPEATED MY DINNER OR breakfast—Krispies, grapes and milk. I love fruit, but for some reason, I hate strawberries in cereal. I like it with raisins, cranberries, peaches or—most of all—green grapes.

While I ate, I leafed through Harley's phone book. It was a nice gesture on his part to give it to me, but all it had in it were names and numbers. No indication what the person did. He already knew all that stuff. Harley was going to have no choice but to live long enough to fill me in on everybody in the book. I now had two books that were, to a certain extent, unreadable for me.

But he did tell me to call Chummy and I found him—of all places—under "C." That's all it said: Chummy and the phone number.

I dialed.

The phone rang five times. Most answer machines pick up after three or four rings. When it reached five, I decided just to let it ring. I counted 12 when it was finally picked up.

"Yuh?" The voice was very faint.

"Chummy?"

There was a pause, then, "Who wantsta know?" Slightly stronger.

"Harley told me to call you if I needed help."

"Where is Harley?" Chummy asked, his voice suddenly louder. "Ain't seen him lately."

"He's in the hospital."

"What for?"

I hesitated, then figured telling the truth was the way to go. "He's got cancer."

"Oh, hell," Chummy said. It got silent and for a moment I thought he hung up. Then: "How bad?"

"Very bad."

"Shit," he said. "Harley's good people."

"He's the best."

Another pause, and then he said, "You must be Auggie."

"I am," I said, "but what made you think so?"

"Harley wouldn't give my number ta nobody else," he said. "So you need Chummy's help, huh?"

"Well," I said, "I have a problem that Harley said you could help me with. I actually don't really know what you do."

"And I ain't about ta tell y'all on the phone," he said. "Let's meet."

"Where?"

"Someplace we can get a beer and no music. A dive bar."

"The Basement, on South Eighth."

"That ain't no dive bar, and they got music."

"At night," I said.

"Naw, naw, meet me at Brown's Diner, on Blair."

"I know it." It was a locals bar, no tourists, with a line cook flipping burgers.

"Okay, meet me there in an hour. I got somethin' else I gotta get out of, first."

"That's early," I said. "Will they be open?"

"Open and servin' beer and burgers for breakfast," he said, proudly.

"Okay. Thanks, Chummy. How will I know you?"

"You ever been to Brown's before?"

"Once or twice."

"But you ain't a regular."

"No."

"Then I'll know you, kid," he said and hung up.

Whatever Chummy did I knew it had to be illegal. Harley had a cadre of them that he used when he needed help.

I looked out my window, trying to see if Hollinger or Lewis were on the block. I didn't want them following me to Brown's, and I didn't trust myself to know if I was being followed. I was just going to have to try taking some evasive action and hope it either worked or wasn't necessary.

29

Brown's was in a neighborhood called Hillsboro West End, or HWEN. They even had a HWEN website, with a gift shop.

It was mostly residential, but Brown's had been in business for a long time. The residents ate and drank there, and were comfortable. They were uncomfortable when a stranger walked in. I qualified.

I entered, drew stares from the men sitting at the bar, their heads hanging over their beer. The smell of frying meat hung in the air. You ate your burgers well done, or you didn't eat at Brown's. The line cook glanced over, but then went back to his burgers.

"Auggie!"

I turned my head, saw a man hanging out of a cracked leather booth. He waved at me. That was all it took to clear me with the others, and they went back to their drinks. As I walked, I noticed the men at the bar had lots of hair. On their heads and face, it made me—with my bald head and clean-shaven face—the oddity.

"Set yourself down," the man said when I reached the booth. "I'm Chummy."

Chummy had a mustache, no beard, and a head of thinning hair that was long in the back. When he extended his hands, I saw that the fingers were long, slender, graceful. He wasn't muscle. Those hands worked with tools—small tools.

I sat down, looked out the window.

"You got yerself some trouble?"

"Some."

"Anybody followin' you?"

I looked out the window a little longer, then turned toward him. "No," trying to sound confident.

"Want a burger and a beer?"

"Sure." Breakfast of champions.

He waved a hand, and that seemed to be enough.

"Take you a minute," he said, "and tell me 'bout Harley."

I told him everything Harley had told me, everything I had found out from the doctors.

"Man, that truly sucks," he said when I was finished.

"Yeah."

"And he won't put up a fight at all?"

"Doesn't see the point."

"Shitfire," he said, "I'd hang on for dear life. I'm goin' to my grave kickin' and screamin', that's for goldurn sure."

"I guess that's how most people feel."

The line cook was apparently also the waiter. He brought us our burgers, stacked high with onions and cheese. Thick cut fries that glistened with oil and two mugs of beer rounded out the meal.

Chummy picked up the salt shaker and covered his fries. His age was hard to tell. His face was lined, his hair thinning, but his hands were smooth. I picked up a fry and bit into it. They were remarkably good for being so greasy.

"They's better with salt," he said, pushing the shaker over.

He was right. I bit into my burger, also good.

"Okay, so what's y'all's problem?" he asked. "Workin' your own case?"

"You don't know the half of it."

I explained to him how I had gotten myself into this mess.

"Geez, you really are workin' on your own case," he said. "You know you ain't gonna come out of this with what ya want, don't ya?"

"How do you mean?"

"Big shots like this feller Corky are real good at danglin' that carrot in front of your face, but they ain't real good at lettin' you catch it."

It was something I had been thinking myself. I was probably going to have to be satisfied with getting myself out from under the police's suspicion. Corky and Rutlidge would most likely screw me out of a record deal.

"I know it."

"Okay, then," he said. "Just didn't want ya bein' surprised when it happened. So whataya want me to do for ya, son?"

"Harley said I have to get a look inside that storage unit," I said. "That's when he said I should call you."

"Locks." His eyes lit up. "They's my specialty."

"Harley's good at them."

"He's good," Chummy said, "but I'm a dang expert. He uses me when he cain't get the job done hisself."

"Well, I'm kind of floundering out here, Chummy," I said. "I need some guidance."

"Sounds to me like you been goin' about it the right way, so far. Part of knowin' what you're doin' is knowin' when ya don't know what you're doin' and ya need help."

"It's kind of scary," I said, "but I think I understood that."

"I can help you with locks," he said, "I cain't help you run your investigation. But y'all are a smart kid. You'll figure it out."

"I hope so."

"When you wanna do this thang?"

"Tonight, I guess. Sooner the better."

"Well, eat up," Chummy said. "I'll hafta take a look at the sitch-e-ation myself, so I know what tools to bring along."

"Do I have to do that with you?" I asked.

"Well, no, not if yer a might squeamish about creepin' a place, but—"

"No, no," I said, "I'll be there when we break in. I just thought I could get some others things done while you scout the place out."

"Oh well, sure," he said. "After all, you do got an investigation to run, don't ya?"

"I do at that."

"Well," he said, "eat up. Ain't right ta let yer breakfast go to waste."

ANDY PAC WAS NOT HARD TO SPOT. I WAGERED WITH myself that, in Nashville, he was the only Asian who worked at Starcade Records.

He came out of the building at noon, I assumed for lunch. He was about five-six, with black hair and black-rimmed eyeglasses, in shirtsleeves and a loosened tie. I left the doorway I was in across the street and followed him. He walked briskly to West End Avenue and went into the Tin Angel. Regulars loved the pressed tin ceiling, the delicious food, and the fact that tourists didn't patronize the Angel.

I stopped just inside the front door. Pac was shown to a table and handed a menu.

I walked to the table, pulled out the chair across from him and sat down.

"Hey, Andy, how's it goin'?"

He lowered the menu and frowned over it at me. His cologne wafted across the table and I wrinkled my nose.

"Do I know you?" he asked.

"I hope so," I said. "Auggie Velez."

Pac put his menu down and pointed at me. "Session man right? Guitar?"

"That's right."

"You do some harmony, and . . . write songs, don't you?"

"Right, again."

"Yeah, yeah," Pac said, warming to the subject, "you wrote that song, the one that goes—"

"Okay, yeah," I said, cutting him off. "I did, but let's not go there."

"So how are you?" he asked. "Here for lunch?"

Still full from my hamburger breakfast I said, "I'm actually here to talk to you, Andy."

"Me? About what?"

"Look, if it's all right with you," I said, "I'll have some coffee while you eat. I'm sure you've got like an hour, right?"

"Right," he said. "That's why I come here. The service is quick, and the food is good."

"So, go ahead and order," I said, "and then we can talk."

"Well . . ." he shrugged. "Okay. Lemme look." He picked up the menu again.

I hoped when he found out what I wanted to talk about that I wouldn't run into a brick wall of loyalty to Corky and Starcade Records. Or maybe I could convince him that it was in the best interest of both to talk to me.

He ordered while I was deep in thought, so I didn't hear what he'd chosen. When the waitress looked at me, I told her I'd just have coffee.

As she walked away, Pac looked at me and said, "What's on your mind, Auggie? You know I don't sign talent, right, I just—"

"No, no, it's not about that," I said. "I'm already working for Corky."

"Is that a fact? He signed you?"

"Not exactly."

Pac looked confused. "Then what's this about?" He pointed to our surroundings. "This wasn't a coincidence, was it?"

"No, it wasn't. I followed you here."

"You followed me?"

"I need your help."

"With what?"

"Corky hired me to find something he lost."

"And what would that be?"

"I'm afraid that has to be confidential," I said, "unless Corky decides to clue you in."

"Is Rutlidge in on this?" Pac asked.

"He is. He's the one who called me."

"Of course," Pac said. "Those two are asshole buddies from way back." Pac didn't seem to like being left on the outside.

"Does the name Felix Nolan mean anything to you?" I asked.

"Nolan?" He frowned. "No, I don't know that name. Who is he?"

"I . . . can't say," I replied.

"Look, I don't like this," Pac said. "You follow me, butt in on my lunch, expect me to answer questions, but you don't tell me anything."

It was obvious Corky and Rutlidge had kept Pac out of the Felix Nolan business. As a result, it was doubtful the man could tell me anything.

"I guess this was a bad idea," I said, pushing my chair back. "I apologize for interrupting your lunch."

"Now, look here," Pac said, "I have some questions of my own—"

"I think you better aim those questions at your boss, Andy," I said, wondering what would happen if and when he did. Would I get canned for talking to him?

"Hey, you can't—"

"Sorry, Andy," I said. "I gotta go. Enjoy your lunch."

I hustled out of the place while he was still sputtering.

I LEFT THE TIN ANGEL AND CHECKED MY WATCH. Chummy might have had time enough to check out the storage unit, but he'd promised to call when he knew something. I figured I had time to go and check on Harley in the hospital.

I took out my cell phone and it rang in my hand.

"Hello?"

"You got your car?" Harley asked.

"I can go and get it."

"Well, do that and then come and get me."

"They're releasing you?"

"I'm goin' home," Harley said. "Come and get me. I'll be waitin' out front."

"I'll be there."

I HAD to go back home to get my car, then drive to the hospital. Harley was sitting on a bench out front. When I pulled up, he stood and started shuffling toward my car. I turned to get out of the car to help him, then thought better of it. If he really needed help, he would have waved to me.

He reached the car, leaned on it, opened the passenger side door and eased himself slowly inside. As he settled into the seat, he moaned.

"Okay?" I asked.

He slammed the door and said, "Drive."

"Home?"

"Zackie's."

"Harley—"

"I need a hot dog, Auggie," he rasped. "Then you can take me home."

I started the car.

WHEN WE GOT to Zackie's, I got out and bought him a hot dog and a Coke.

"None for you?" he asked, as I got in the car and handed it to him. I put the Coke in a cup holder.

"I had breakfast with Chummy."

"Hey, how'd you get along with him?" he asked, around his first bite.

"Good, I guess. He's gonna help me out."

"That's good. Ain't a locked door he can't handle. Or a safe. You gotta break into a safe?"

"I don't think so. At least, I hope not."

"Well, whatever he does for you make sure you go and watch. Then maybe you can do it yerself, next time."

"I'm hoping there won't be a next time."

Harley laughed, then choked. He was careful not to waste any hotdog, though. He sipped his Coke, then took another bite.

"Now that you've had a real case of your own, you'll be

hooked. No more serving papers for you, Auggie. You're a real private dick, now."

"Well . . . let's give that some time, Harley." I'd had my license for a while, but was still working for Harley. Considering his condition, maybe it was time I started taking my own cases.

"Naw, you'll see," Harley said. "It gets down inside of ya."

"I'm gonna take you home, now," I said. "Then I've got to go meet Chummy."

"I'd come with ya, kid," Harley said, "but I'm kinda tired."

His hot dog was gone, and he had nodded off by the time I pulled up in front of his house. I hated to wake him, but I wasn't about to carry him inside.

As it turned out, I half dragged-half carried him, anyway, deposited him on his sofa, right into the depression he'd worn into one of the cushions.

"Anything else I can do for you, Harley?" I asked.

"Naw, I'm good." He burped, then drifted off, his head back.

I checked my cell for messages. I had one missed call. When I played it back, it was Chummy.

"Checked it out, kid. Shouldn't be too hard. I won't come by your place 'cause you said the cops was watchin' ya'll. I'll just meet ya out there around ten P.M. Wear dark clothes and sneakers. They still call 'em sneaker? I do. See ya'll."

Okay, so I had nothing to do until 10 P.M. My inter-view with Andy Pac had yielded nothing. And all I'd gotten from Felix Nolan's apartment was the book I couldn't make heads or tails of. I wished I'd found a phone book, but the cops had probably taken that.

Wait a minute. Corky and Rutlidge had given me Nolan's cell number. All I had to do was get a copy of his bill, then check out the numbers he'd called the most to find somebody who knew something.

Now the question was, could I get a look at a record if his calls?

Harley's book, which I had left at home.

I checked him to make sure he was breathing okay, then left to drive back to my place.

32

I DRESSED IN A BLACK SLASH T-SHIRT (WITH A GIBSON Les Paul guitar), black jeans, and running shoes. I didn't wear them to run, but once in a while, I used them to shoot some hoops.

I drank a cup of coffee looking out my window, trying to spot somebody watching my place. Since I wasn't the pro the cops were, there was little chance I'd see them if they didn't want me to. I was just going to have to hope that when I drove to meet Chummy, I'd be able to lose anyone who might be following me.

I had returned home after leaving Harley's. (I didn't see anyone outside, but that didn't mean they weren't there.) I went through his book, started to see that Harley had his own code—not quite as convoluted as the one in Nolan's book. For instance, next to Chummy's name he had a capital "L," which I assumed stood for "Locks." I found a few names with a "P," but after a couple of calls it became clear that did not stand for "phone." Especially when one of the numbers turned out to be a porno bookshop. (Pretty clear what "P" stood for after that.)

I found a girl's name with a "C" next to it. In this day and age, I was hoping it stood for "Computers." I got lucky. Not only did Ellen work on computers, but she told me she'd done computer checks for Harley before.

"You won't ever see the day when Harley'll sit in front of a computer," she said. "How is he? I haven't heard from him in a while."

I had two motives for telling her about Harley's bout with cancer. First, to answer her question, but second to get her in the mood to help me out.

"Oh jeez," she said, "that sounds awful. Can I send him somethin'?

"You got his home address?"

"Yes, I do."

"Sure, go ahead," I said. "I'm sure he'll be happy to hear from you."

"Well, is there something he'd like me to look up? Is that the reason you called?"

I'd told her I worked with Harley. So whatever I asked her for, she'd think it was for him.

"There's a cell number we need some records for."

"Oh, sure, I can do that easy. How many months' worth?"

"Just this one, and last month," I said.

"Print out? Or should I email them?"

"You can email them, but to my computer," I said. "Harley's gonna be resting for a while."

"Oh, sure," she said. "Just give me your email, and I'll get this to you by tonight or tomorrow morning."

"That's cool. Thanks."

"Um, I feel bad for Harley and all, but I will have to charge regular price . . . I mean, I've got to make a living . . ."

"No problem Ellen," I said. "Just tell me in the email how much and where to send it."

"Great! And I'll send him a card."

"Cool," I said. "Thanks."

"No prob," she said and hung up.

I SPENT a few hours with my Little Martin, working on some tunes. Not that I believed Corky that he was ever going to record me. I'd pretty much given up on that carrot. But songwriting relaxes me, and I didn't want to just sit around thinking about my first real attempt at breaking and entering. (Well, except for Nolan's apartment.)

I worked on some melodies that had been going through my head for a few days. I wanted to get them down before I tried to put lyrics to them. I find I start a lot of songs that I don't finish. That doesn't bother me. One of my favorite quotes about songwriting comes from Johnny Cash. He said, "I start a lot more sings than I finish because I realize when I get into them, they're no good. I don't throw them away, I just put them away, store them, get them out of sight." I don't know where Johnny put them, but I have a box filled with parts of songs. Every once in a while I'll take one out and finish it—or try to.

At nine-thirty I put my guitar aside and walked to the front window. It was dark out, so I had even less hope of seeing someone unless they were in an apartment across the way. Those windows were dark, but I stared for a few minutes, hoping for the glow of a cigarette tip, or something. There was nothing there, though, except my paranoia.

I put on a bandana that completely covered my bald

head and left. I had parked my car on the street around the corner, risking a ticket. At least I had lucked out in that department. I got behind the wheel, started the engine, and sat there for a few minutes, watching the rearview mirror. When I pulled away from the curb, I was pretty sure no one was following me—but I wasn't positive. I zig-zagged through some of the city streets, hoping it would be enough, and then headed to East Germantown to meet Chummy.

IT WAS dark on Adams Street. The Jazz Workshop across the street was dark, as well, so no late-night concerts or lessons were going on.

I parked in front of the Workshop, walked across the street to the storage unit. By my watch, it was 10:05 P.M.

PART 3

"I'm pickin' the lock on your heart . . ."

Edgar "Chummy" Grimes

33

I DIDN'T SEE CHUMMY, BUT I HEARD HIM SINGING. Then he stepped out of the shadows. He was dressed all in black, including leather gloves.

"You write songs, right?" he asked.

"That's right." I wondered what that had to do with the task at hand.

"I got some tunes," he said. "I'll let ya see them someday."

"Uh, okay."

"This here ain't gonna be hard," he said, indicating the storage unit. "There ain't no security, and the light ain't so good." He pointed to a lone yellow blub that couldn't have been more than 40 watts. "Come on; I'll show ya."

I followed him to the locked front gate.

"This here's got a keypad. You need to punch in your code to get in."

"So how do we get in?"

"Well, I can bypass the electronic lock by breaking the connection," he said.

"How would you do that?"

"I got me my own card for that," Chummy said. "I just slide it in and break the connection, making the electronic lock snap open."

"Okay."

"Or," he said, "I kin do this."

He stepped to the keypad, punched in four numbers. There was a snapping sound and the gate began to slide open sideways, on wheels.

"How did you do that?" I asked.

"People get to pick their own codes," he said, "and somebody always picks Christmas. One-two-two-five. Hurry, let's get inside."

We slipped in and then I noticed the gate closing behind us.

"Is it supposed to do that?" I asked.

"Don't worry," he said. "We'll be able to get out. Come on. You got the unit number?"

A cold feeling settled in the pit of my stomach. Did I make us come all this way without the unit number? I pulled the storage bill out of my pocket and unfolded it. Thankfully, the number was on it.

"Four-seventeen," I said.

We walked around the buildings, looking at the numbers. They were all outdoor units with metal doors that slid upward. Luckily, when we found it, we were between buildings, where we could not be seen from the street. Chummy's comment about the lights was an understatement—there was no light.

"We're lucky we're not dealin' with a downtown unit," he said. "They'd be lit up like a birthday cake, plus there'd be security."

"How are we going to—" before I could say "see" he switched on a small flashlight.

In the strong beam of his small light, we spotted the lock. It was a simple padlock, the key to which was probably on a keychain with Nolan's personal effects in the police lock-up.

"You gotta hol' the light," Chummy said.

He handed me the penlight and took out his lock picks. While he worked, he started to sing under his breath. "I'm pickin' the loooock . . . on your heart . . . hopin' . . . to open . . . your love . . ."

The melody was the old Roy Rogers theme "Happy Trails to You." I suspected the lyrics were his own.

The lock snapped open, and he slipped it off the door.

Grabbing the door at the bottom, he pulled it open slowly, so that the metal wouldn't make a lot of noise.

"There ya go," he said. "You coulda done this one."

"Right," I said, "but I'd probably still be outside the gate."

He turned and looked at me. "If you had started just punchin' in numbers I bet ya woulda got it open."

"This was faster," I said. "Thanks, Chummy."

We stepped inside the dark interior of the unit. It looked to be five by ten feet wide, ten feet deep.

"What are we lookin' for?" he asked in a low voice.

"If nobody's around why are we whisperin'?" I asked.

"It's a good habit to get into if yer gonna do this kind of work."

I didn't tell him that I hoped never to have to do this again.

I moved the flashlight around. Light bounced off of many boxes, a couple of bookcases against the walls with books and boxes on them. In a corner were some instrument cases.

"Do we wanna open some of these up?"

"I guess we might as well," I said, "since we're here. But what I'm really looking for would fit into an attaché case."

"Okay."

Chummy took out a second flashlight for himself. I was impressed by how prepared he was, but Harley had said he was the best at what he did.

While we were looking in boxes—most of which seemed to be filled with papers and books that had to do with music—Chummy started singing his song again. The more I listened, the more I realized the lyrics weren't that bad. Or I was getting punchy.

"I'm tryin' ta unlooooock your love . . ." he sang, off-key.

He stopped suddenly, leaned over and asked, "A case like this?"

I turned, shone my light on the case he was holding.

"Jesus," I said, "that's it."

"You sure?" he asked. "Could just look like it."

"Hold it up."

He held it out in both hands so I could shine my light over the whole thing.

"No, I remember this scuff mark right here."

"That's good," he said. "Ya gotta notice everythin' in this business."

He turned it around so the front was facing me.

"Let's open it," he suggested.

I reached for the locks.

34

I DON'T WATCH MUCH TV, BUT RECENTLY I CAUGHT A show called Storage Wars while I was home sick with the flu for a week. As I reached for the locks on the case, I knew how those guys felt on that show. You just never knew what kind of treasure you're going to find.

I moved the catches; the locks flipped open. I lifted the lid while Chummy peered over it with interest.

Empty.

"Well," Chummy said, "that would've been too dang easy."

"Yeah, well, I would've taken easy, at this point."

I closed the case and Chummy set it on the ground.

"Let's keep lookin'," he suggested.

We did, but didn't find anything. After a couple of hours, we called it quits. My hands were coated with dust and grime, making me wish I had thought to bring gloves, as Chummy had.

"I'm done," I said, finally. "There's nothing in here to tell us who killed Felix Nolan, or what was in the case."

"There's lots of music here," Chummy pointed out. "This what it looks like when it's all written down?"

He was holding a page of sheet music in his hands.

"That's it."

"That boy write this?"

I looked closer and said, "No, not that. That came out of a book."

"Did he write any of this?"

I opened one of the boxes, saw what looked like some aborted attempts.

"Some of these look like he tried," I told Chummy.

"This looks hard. All these lines, and dots with tails on them . . ."

"Yeah, it's pretty hard," I agreed.

"This what you do?"

"Kind of," I said. "I'm not real good at actually writing music, so I work with somebody else to do that once I get the song down in my head."

"Like a partner?"

"Yes, like a partner."

We stepped out of the unit and Chummy pulled the door closed, set the lock back in place. That was when I saw he was holding the attaché case.

"Why'd you take that?" I asked.

"You been lookin' for it," he said. "I thought you'd wanna take it home."

I almost told him that what I was looking for had been inside the case, but instead, I said, "Why not? I'll take it."

We walked back to the gate and Chummy punched in the Christmas Day numbers. The gate opened and we stepped out. It was close to midnight.

"I'm hungry," Chummy said, "you hungry?"

"Yeah," I said, realizing my stomach had been growling for a while, "I'm hungry."

WE WERE NEAR KNOCK-OUT Wings in Germantown, which was where Chummy wanted to go. I suggested the Paradise Park Trailer Resort, but he tumbled to the fact that I picked the place because it was downtown and closer to home for me. He then mentioned MafiaOza's, which was in Berry Hills and close to where he lived. As tempting as mason jars of beer was, we finally agreed on Knock-Out Wings which was open till 2 A.M.

WE GOT SITUATED with a huge plate of wings and beers in the middle of the table. We settled on a mix of respectably hot and lemon pepper wings. Add to that their great honey biscuits and we were both pretty happy.

"So," Chummy asked with hot sauce smeared around his mouth, "what's next?"

"I don't know," I said. I'd searched Nolan's apartment, talked with Andy Pac, and searched the storage unit. I literally didn't know what to do next.

"Are the cops really tryin' ta fit you for this?"

"I don't know," I said. "They've talked to me a few times."

"They lookin' at anybody else?"

"I don't know that, either."

"When did this murder happen?"

"Weeks ago."

"Ya know what I think?"

"What?"

"You should go back to your life. Forget about this. If they was gonna arrest ya, they probably woulda by now."

"You think?"

"Somebody payin' ya to investigate this?"

"Well . . . yeah."

"Them record people?"

I nodded.

"Can't trust them," he said. "Tell 'em ta stuff it. Go back ta your music. Take one of them—whatayacallit—wait-and-see attitudes."

Yeah, I thought, wait-and-see if they're going to arrest me.

WE FINISHED EATING and decided to have one more beer each before we left.

"Anything else I can do to help?" he asked.

"I don't think I have any more breaking-and-entering to do," I said. "If I do I'll give you a call."

"No other clues that maybe me or Harley could help with?" Chummy asked.

"Clues," I said, shaking my head. "That's just it. There aren't many clues. I searched Nolan's apartment—all I came up with was this."

I took from my pocket the book I'd found in Nolan's place and put it on the table. Chummy picked it up and leafed through it.

"What're these numbers?"

"That's just it. I don't know. All I know so far is that they're not phone numbers."

"Maybe they're account numbers," Chummy said. "Ya know? For banks?"

"Could be. I'll need to find somebody to ask, though. Somebody good with codes."

I reached for the book, but Chummy pulled it away from me.

"How about you leave it with me?"

"Why? You good at codes?"

"Me? Naw, math ain't my thing. But I did a job for a guy a few years back. He's good at codes. Maybe I can get him to look at it."

"Well . . . okay, sure," I said. "Tell him as much or as little as you can."

"Yeah, okay." Chummy put the book in his pocket, finished his beer. We paid the bill and walked outside.

I offered to send him a check for his help.

"I don't do checks, kid," he said, "and I did this for Harley. You make sure he knows. But you need me in the future, we can talk price. Okay?"

"Okay, Chummy. Thanks."

We shook hands and went our separate ways.

35

I DROVE HOME, THINKING OVER CHUMMY'S ADVICE about the wait-and-see attitude. As far as I was concerned my "investigation" was at a standstill. Maybe wait-and-see was the best way to go. Or maybe his code guy would give me a way to go.

When I got home I scanned the street for anyone watching me, then went upstairs. I unlocked my door and hurried inside, flicking the lights on right away. As far as I could see—or feel—nobody had been there in my absence.

I was beat. I washed up and hit the sack. Once I was between the sheets, I forgot all about Felix Nolan, Corky Barnes and the cops.

THE NEXT MORNING, over coffee and toast, I checked my schedule, reminding myself that I still had to make a living. It was a good thing I did because I had a gig that night at the Rum Boogie Café on Beale Street in Memphis. Damn, I'd almost let this stupid case make me miss a job.

That was all I had to do, not show up for a gig. My name would be mud in Tennessee after that.

I checked my watch: 9 A.M. I was supposed to be on stage at the Boogie at 5 P.M., playing guitar and singing backup for a fairly new artist. It was about a three-hour drive, and if I got there early enough they'd feed me; being fed was no small part of these club gigs, believe me.

I figured I'd leave about 2 P.M., beat rush hour out of Nashville, catch a bit of it into Memphis, but not too bad. The artist was a girl who was being touted as "Taylor Swift with soul." She didn't have her own band yet, so a few guys and I were getting together to back her up. I'd have to break out my best jeans and bandana for this one. But Rum Boogie wasn't the only thing on my calendar. Nashville hosted many events and festivals during the year, and October was full of them. The events I was concerned with were the Americana Music Festival, scheduled for October 12-15. A succession of concert and parties, panel discussions and workshops led up to the Americana Honors & Awards, which would be taking place on October 13 at the Ryman Auditorium. I had agreed to play a few gigs during the week, including a couple at the Ryman on awards night. I couldn't afford to let this murder interfere with that. I'm a man who honors my commitments—which I would not be able to do from prison!

In addition to the Americana events, October marked the 86th birthday of the Grand Ole Opry (events October 7-8), and Germantown was going to be hosting their 31st annual Oktoberfest on October 8th. I didn't have any commitments there, but I wanted to go. In addition, the following week I had a few session gigs. These were the things I had marked on my calendar for October, and nowhere did it say anything about getting involved with a murder.

AFTER A WHILE, I made a decision and called Allegra.

"I thought you forgot about me," she said playfully.

"How could I do that?" I asked. "We spent a memorable night together."

"Which you barely remember."

"And you remember every moment?"

She hesitated, then admitted, "I remember a blissful moment, or two."

"Are you at work?" I asked.

"I'm unemployed, remember? Still haven't found a job. Why?"

"I have a gig at a club on Beale Street in Memphis," I said. "Thought you might like to come."

"With you?"

"Yes, with me. I'll pick you up and everything. Even drive you home after."

"What time?"

I told her.

"Okay," she said "Pick me up. What should I wear?"

"We're going to a club called the Rum Boogie."

"Gotcha," she said. "See you later."

SINCE GETTING OFF THE BUS, I had been going round and round on this murder thing I got dragged into by Corky Barnes and Walter Rutlidge. But was it all their fault? Sure, they'd lied to me—by omission, maybe—but I'd gone back a second time, and a second time had taken money, grabbing for that damn carrot. At this point, I was in it more because of me than because of them. I'd had my out, and I didn't take it.

Dumb.

When somebody gives you an out, the simple fact that you are *viewing* it as an out means you should take it.

Of course, if I decided to chuck the whole thing, leave it to the police and see what they came up with, did that mean I had to give the money back to Corky Barnes? Not the first payment. I had earned that one by delivering the case. But the second five thousand, which he gave me for finding—or trying to find—the case and bringing it back?

All I had to do was tell him I *tried* to find it and failed. If I put it that way, wasn't I entitled to keep the money?

Without feeling like a scumbag?

36

THE RUM BOOGIE SPECIALIZED IN BEER AND RUM drinks. A friend of mine, Tad Colvin, agreed to back up the singer when her manager booked her there. He played bass, had a drummer and a keyboard player. He recruited me to play rhythm guitar and do backup vocals and harmony when needed.

I picked up Allegra and we got better acquainted during the ride, exchanging bits of history, but I doubted either one of us had dug deep yet. For instance, I told her nothing about Afghanistan. I usually saved that for people I knew were going to be in my life for a long time, like Elton and Harley.

When we got there Tad was busy getting set up. We did a sound check, rehearsed for half an hour, and then they fed us.

"Be nice if the star of the hour was here to rehearse with us," I said. Tad had stood in for her. Hopefully harmonizing with him had prepared me to do the same with her.

I introduced Allegra to Tad and the other guys. She

was wearing a short dress that clung to her, revealing the fact that she did not have an ounce of fat on her. She told me it was made of some material that didn't wrinkle, even if she had rolled it up and put it into her big purse. I wondered if that was her way of telling me she had another one tucked away.

We went through more than a few rum/beer drinks and were pretty loose by the time the girl arrived with her manager.

"Hello, Tad," the man said.

"Eddie," Tad said. "You know Bill and Froggie. This is Auggie Velez, and his friend, Allegra."

"Hello, Auggie," Eddie Tayback said. I knew his reputation. He was not a top of the line manager, but he thought he had something here with this little lady, Evie Maxwell. Tayback was close to fifty now, his red hair thinning, making his big ears look even bigger. He used to make his girl singers pay him with a percentage and hummers, but maybe he was getting too old for that. He smirked at Allegra and gave her a smarmy hello.

"Hey, Eddie. Where's your girl?" I asked.

"She's on her way in," Eddie said. "I got some people to stop her outside for autographs."

Autographs, I thought. The girl didn't even have a song on iTunes yet. Wouldn't she be suspicious about people wanting her autograph?

"We need to check her levels, Eddie," Tad said. He was never happy with divas, and Eddie seemed to be grooming his girl that way.

"She'll be right in, Tad," Eddie said. "Don't you worry. I got her trained."

"Yeah, yeah," Tad said.

We did some last-minute tuning while the house began

to fill up. I wondered how many of these people had been sent in by Eddie because there wasn't going to be an empty seat in the house. I was glad I'd gotten Allegra a table down front, where she was sitting alone.

And then I saw him at a table about halfway back, with a woman. Detective Hollinger stared up at me with a benign smile.

I wondered what I should do and finally decided just to play it head on. I put my guitar down, worked my way between tables until I got to his.

"Hello, Auggie."

"Detective," I said. "I don't guess this is much of a coincidence."

"No, it isn't," Hollinger said. "I'm really curious about what you do, so I thought I'd come and have a listen."

"And this pretty lady?"

"Oh, sorry. This s my wife, Tracy, who is always telling me I have no manners."

"Hello, Mr. Velez," she said.

"Please," I said, "it's just Auggie." She was in her thirties, pretty in a housewifey way. As a cop's wife, I guessed she was used to being in some awkward situations, but she seemed very comfortable.

"Auggie, I've never heard of this girl. Is she any good?"

"Tracy, I try not to have opinions about people who are paying me to back them up."

"Oh? Don't you only do it for people you like?"

"That's not the way it works when you do this for a living," I said, "and you're not Garth Brooks. I'm afraid I play for whoever pays me. The gigs I take just for the love of the music are few and far between."

"That must make them that much more enjoyable."

"Exactly." I looked at Hollinger. "She's pretty smart."

"Except she decided to marry me," Hollinger said. "The jury is still out on how smart that was."

"How long have you been married?" I asked.

"Fifteen years," he said.

"That's a long time for a jury to deliberate."

"They're very close to a decision, though," she said, putting her hand on her husband's arm. I could see she clearly adored him.

A loud, sour note from the stage alerted me to the fact that my presence was desired.

"I hope you enjoy the show," I said to them both. "I have to go."

"Nice to meet you, Auggie."

"You, too, Tracy."

I turned and hurried back toward the stage, where Evie was playing with the mike stand. It hadn't occurred to me then to ask Hollinger how he knew I'd be there. Maybe he was just a good detective.

"Is there a problem, Auggie?" Allegra asked.

"No problem. Show's about to start."

I stopped and helped Evie adjust the mike to her height. She didn't even acknowledge me with a nod.

I picked up my guitar and watched Tad for my cue.

EVIE DID SOME COVERS—TAYLOR Swift, Carrie Underwood stuff, like that—but also did some original tunes that reminded me of a Kellie Pickler concert.

There was no denying Evie's voice had some raw power, but she was going to need fine tuning and—in the end—probably somebody else to handle her if she was going to go anywhere.

Tad had coached me on her original tunes, but luckily there were only two and the rest were covers.

The night went really well, I thought, aside for a momentary mike malfunction and a two-minute sound system glitch. (Tad's fault, not the Rum Boogie's.)

But then somebody in the audience went and done it.

"Do 'Stan the Pool Man,'" a voice called out.

People laughed, and then started clapping rhythmically. As usual, I could feel my face flush. Nobody on stage knew what to say until Evie turned to us and said happily, "I know that one!"

It figured.

37

I MUMBLED SOMETHING TO THE CROWD ABOUT BEING prohibited from playing that song because of copyright infringement. A few diehards tried to rouse the crowd by clapping and stamping their feet, but they soon quit and people went back to their drinks.

"Be back in a while," Evie said into the mike and took a break. We had a second set, but we'd have time for a few drinks before then. Evie needed to loosen up a bit. She was too tense up there.

The band sat with me and Allegra; we all drank. Both Evie and Eddie disappeared, so I assumed Eddie was collecting his fifteen percent in the back somewhere.

I also decided to be the big man and buy a round of drinks for Detective Hollinger and his wife. Hollinger looked around until he spotted me, and waved his thanks. I waved back. Very civilized.

Just before the second set Hollinger and his wife got up and left. I didn't take offense since they had to drive back to Nashville—unless they were having a romantic night at a Memphis Hotel, maybe the Peabody around the corner.

The guys drifted away after a while, to the bar or the bathroom, leaving me with Allegra.

"I didn't know you wrote 'Stan the Pool Man,'" she said.

"And I would've kept it from you if some fool hadn't shot off his big mouth."

"Why? Are you ashamed? It was a hit."

"A novelty hit. The poor guy who recorded it the first time is now known as a One-Hit-Wonder."

"But it's been recorded since then. Wasn't it the theme of a TV series?"

"Oh God," I said, putting my head in my hands.

"I thought everyone wanted to have a hit record."

"I'd prefer to have a real hit—and more than one. I hate being in the same category as the 'Macarena' and 'Gangnam Style.'"

"I'm sorry," she said. "I didn't think it was a sore point. I won't bring it up again."

"No, I'm sorry," I said. "You had no way of knowing that. It's okay."

Evie came over and sat down with us. I felt bad that I couldn't look at her without seeing her on her knees in front of Eddie.

"I didn't know you wrote the pool man song," she said.

Allegra hunched her shoulders and sipped her drink. Evie hadn't acknowledged her presence anyway.

"Yeah, well," I said, "it's not something I brag about."

"But that was epic!"

"In its day," I said, "and for all the wrong reasons."

"What did you think of my songs?" she asked. "You learned 'em pretty quick."

"I rehearsed with Tad earlier," I said.

I didn't know where she was from, but there was not the slightest hint of a southern accent. Maybe the Midwest.

"You want a drink?" I asked her.

"Sure."

I called a waitress over and bought her a drink. She asked for a screwdriver. I was surprised the waitress didn't card her.

"You play pretty good," Evie said.

"Thanks."

"I'm learnin'. Eddie says I'll look better up there holdin' a guitar."

"Well, Eddie . . ." I started, and I couldn't think of anything nice to say about him. "Eddie knows his stuff" just wouldn't come out.

"I know Eddie's not a top of the line manager, but I couldn't get anybody else to take me on."

"It's a tough business."

"Who handles you?"

"I book my own gigs," I said.

"Did you ever have a manager?"

"No." I had come to Nashville armed with a couple of names, studio people who liked my references from Austin and other places. It *was* a tough business. I had been able to get myself in the door, make a place for myself, but I wasn't making big money or a big name, and I hadn't been able to move up the ladder much in the past few years. I was pretty much running in place.

"Oh. I thought maybe you might be able to recommend somebody." She seemed crushed that I couldn't.

"Hey," I said, "the Rum Boogie is a good gig. Not just anybody can get in here."

"Yeah?" She brightened.

"Yeah," I said, "you're doing good here."

"Thanks, Auggie."

Eddie appeared behind her then, rested a proprietary hand on her shoulder. I thought I saw her cringe.

"Ready for your second set, baby?" he asked.

"Yeah, Eddie. I'm ready." She smiled wanly at me. "Thanks for the drink, Auggie."

"Sure."

Eddie threw me a dirty look, then took hold of her arm and escorted her to the stage, as if he was afraid she might meet somebody else along the way.

I found myself wishing I could help.

"That guy strikes me as a sleaze," Allegra said.

"You're a good judge of people."

"Am I?" she asked. "Because she strikes me as a real bitch."

The guys went back to their instruments, so I got myself up on stage and grabbed my guitar. Evie turned and looked at me. I thought there was fear in her eyes, but then we got started and she addressed herself to the microphone, the crowd, and the songs.

I never saw her or heard about her, again after that night.

Nice work, Eddie.

38

WE DROVE HOME TO NASHVILLE WITH A BIT OF A BUZZ on. Luckily, I wasn't stopped by any cops. Halfway, Allegra fell asleep with her head on my shoulder. I found it a pleasant experience.

I parked, carried my guitar and dragged my ass up the stairs. She came with me as if there was never any question that she'd be spending the night. When we got to the door I walked in, then suddenly realized I hadn't used my key.

The door had been ajar.

"Stand still," I said.

"What?" she asked, sleepily.

"Shh."

The lights were out. I reached for the wall switches, flicked them. I squinted as the lights blazed, showing a deserted loft—or so I hoped. There weren't too many places to hide if the intruder was still here.

I stood there for a moment, just listening. I could hear music from the Karaoke bar up the street. I looked around to see what was missing, but everything was there.

Everything.

Some of it was just in pieces.

I walked slowly to the far end. My guitars were scattered about like broken bodies after an accident. Only this was no accident. Someone had done a real job on them. They looked as if they'd been stomped on.

I felt empty, devastated . . . and scared.

I turned and said to Allegra, wanting to cry but not daring to in front of her. "Just stay there. Don't move."

"I really have to pee."

I went to the bathroom, flicked the light on and checked it out. It was empty.

"Okay, go ahead. Close the door, and lock it."

"What's going on?"

From her position by the door, she had not been able to see the carnage at the back of the room.

"The door was open, Allegra. I think I got robbed. Just stay in the bathroom while I look around."

"Oh. Okay." She went in and I waited for the sound of the lock.

I looked around, wondering if the intruder might still be present. There were two places to hide—under the bed, or in the one closet I had.

I walked to the bed hesitantly, searching for something to use as a weapon. Finally, I picked up a mike stand that had been knocked over. It was metal, and solid. I went to the bed and, very hesitantly, leaned over to look underneath. I breathed a sigh of relief, seeing nobody there.

Then I carried the mike stand with me to the closet. Holding it in my left hand I used my right to turn the knob slowly, but before I could pull on it, it burst open, hitting me solidly in the face, knocking me backward. I went down, lost my hold on the mike stand as a body came flying out of the closet at me. I got hit again before I could really see anything and found myself in a cloud of cologne as my lights went out. . . .

I HAD NO CHOICE.

Calling the cops was a business decision. It was the only way I'd be able to make a claim on my insurance.

When I woke up, I had no idea how much time had gone by. Checking my watch, I realized it might have only been seconds. I got to my feet with an aching forehead and jaw.

My front door was open. I took a look down the stairs, but of course, no one was there. I went back to my victimized guitars and stared at them while I regained my senses. I still wanted to cry, but even with Allegra in the bathroom, I didn't. Instead grabbed my phone and called 9-1-1.

By the time two uniformed officers responded, Allegra was out of the bathroom, holding a washcloth packed with ice to my forehead. They took my report of a burglary. Or a break-in, since nothing was taken.

"Are you sure nothing's missing, sir?" one of them asked.

"As far as I can tell," I said. "Nothing of any value, anyway."

"And you didn't get a good look at him?"

"I got no look, at all," I said. "He was in the closet, and when I went to open it, he slammed the door open in my face. Then he hit me with something—a knee, I think—and I went out."

His partner had walked around the entire floor and returned to us, shaking his head.

"Too bad about those guitars. Were they expensive?"

"Some of them."

"Well," he said, "let us know what they're worth and we'll put it in the report. Then you can get a copy of the report online and give it to your insurance company." He said insurance with the accent on the first syllable, as people in the Midwest and South did. IN-surance.

"Really?" I asked.

"It's a bold new world, sir," he said.

We went over the guitars and their values.

"Can any of them be saved?" he asked. "Or repaired?"

"I doubt it," I said. "Some parts might be saved, but whoever did this pretty much stomped the shit out of them."

The second man, the older of the two, shook his head again and said, "Too bad. So, you a musician?"

I stared at him for a minute, wondering if he was kidding, and then said, "Yes, I am."

He nodded, then asked, "You ever meet Dolly Parton?"

39

AFTER THE TWO OFFICERS LEFT, I WONDERED IF I'D GET away without this report reaching the detectives. It only took half an hour for me to find out how futile that hope was.

ALLEGRA and I were sitting on my sofa with a beer each, just staring at the floor. She had a hand on my back, trying to soothe me when there was a knock at the door. I hadn't even had the time to think, to wonder what had happened. Was it a burglar, or was it connected with the job I was doing for Corky Barnes? A warning, maybe? But what was I being warned about? I had just about decided to forget the whole thing and try to figure out a way to keep my fee when another knock came at the door.

I got up, walked to the door and opened it.

"What if it was the burglar coming back?" Detective Hollinger asked as he and his partner entered.

"Screw it," I said. "Let him have what he wants."

Lewis stood with me while Hollinger walked to the back to check out the damage.

"Jesus Christ, what a shame!" he said, loudly.

"Who'd you piss off, Auggie?" Lewis asked.

"Language, Lew," Hollinger said, indicating Allegra, who was still on the sofa.

"Oh, sorry."

"That's Allegra," I said. "These are Detectives Hollinger and Lewis."

"Yo," she said.

"Hey, I remember," Hollinger said. "Cory Barnes's secretary, right?"

"Receptionist," she said.

"Why couldn't it just be a burglar?" I asked.

"Well, according to the officers who took your report," Lewis said, "nothing's missing. Burglars usually steal something."

I looked at Hollinger, who was bent over the Takamine, shaking his head.

"No, nothin's missing that I can tell," I said. "Just damage."

"Damage?" Hollinger said, straightening and looking at us. "This is . . . obliteration."

"Whataya think, Auggie?" Lewis asked.

"About what?"

"About what? About this," Lewis said. "About the guitars, the bump on your forehead, and all this. Somebody mad at you? Jealous boyfriend? Husband?"

"This is deliberate destruction, Auggie," Hollinger said, joining us. "Come on, do you think this is a warning?"

"What kind of warning?"

"Somebody wants you to stay away from the Felix Nolan murder."

"Hey," I said, holding my hands up, "I'm nowhere near the murder."

"Then maybe somebody thinks you've got something they want," Lewis said.

"Like what?"

"Like whatever was in that attaché case you delivered."

The attaché case! I had put it in the closet, and I hadn't thought to check and see if it was still there. If they checked . . .

"How many times do I have to tell you," I asked, "I don't know what was in the case. All I did was deliver it. That's what I was hired to do."

"Oh, that's right," Lewis said, "you never looked inside."

"If you know that, it means you tried to open it," Hollinger said.

"I tried the catches, yeah, to make sure it was locked."

"And if it had opened when you did that?" Lewis asked. "Would you have looked inside?"

"No."

"Wow," he said, "you really are a better man than me."

"I don't really know how much of a compliment that is, do I, Detective?"

"Look, Velez—"

"Why don't you wait for me downstairs, Lew?" Hollinger said. "Let me talk to Auggie."

"You can have him," Lewis said, and left, slamming the door behind him.

"His bad cop is too bad to be believed," I commented.

"Look, you're upset, and you have a right to be," Hollinger said. "You get back from Memphis; you're tired, you walk in on what appears to be a burglary, you get smacked in the head and the jaw and your guitars are destroyed."

"You read that whole report already?" I asked.

"Well—"

"Wait a minute," I said. "You've been waiting for somebody to come after me. You put out the word to notify you when it did? Oh, wait, wait."

"Auggie—"

"You've had somebody watching the place this whole time," I said. "You must know who broke in."

Suddenly, Hollinger looked sheepish.

"Uh, no, we didn't," he said. "I mean, we did, but we pulled them when you left town."

"So you weren't watching my place, you've been watching me."

"Kinda."

"What's that mean?"

"It means you managed to shake my men a couple of times because they weren't really trying all that hard."

"Why not?"

"Auggie, we don't really think you killed Felix Nolan."

"Fine," I said, "then I can stop worrying about being arrested for murder."

"Or we could lock you up for less," Hollinger said. "Several conspiracy charges, aiding and abetting before and after the fact—"

"What fact? There are no facts."

"This is no coincidence," Hollinger said. "This is a message."

"Well then, you better translate for me, because I'm not getting it."

Hollinger opened his mouth, then closed it, thought a moment, then spoke.

"This time some guitars got smashed, and you got a lump on the head—I'd have that checked out, by the way —but next time it could be a lot worse. Next time somebody could get killed. If you've got something you want to tell me, Auggie, now would be the time."

"I'll be careful."

He stared at me, then walked to the door. There he stopped and looked at me again.

"Do you have a gun?"

"What the hell would I be doing with a gun?" I asked. "I'd probably shoot my own foot off."

"You're an Afghan vet, Auggie, so don't pretend like you don't know how to handle a gun."

"I haven't held one since I got back, and I don't want to hold one again. I had enough of that over there."

"Yeah," he said, "yeah, I guess you did." He pointed his finger at me. "You did right to call the cops this time. Next time, call me direct." He looked at Allegra. "Good-night, young lady."

He went out, closing the door soundlessly behind him.

40

I WATCHED FROM A WINDOW WHILE THE TWO detectives got into their car and drove away.

"I better take you home," I said to Allegra. "There's no telling if the guy will come back."

"You can stay at my place, Auggie," she offered.

"No," I said, "I better get back here and . . . clean up."

"I can help."

I smiled at her and said, "I appreciate it, but I think I have to do this myself."

She looked over at my smashed guitars and said, "I understand."

I drove her home, promised to call her soon, and rushed back.

IT WASN'T SO MUCH I had to clean up as I wanted to take a look at that attaché case again, without anyone—even Allegra—knowing I had it. But first I cleaned up the pieces of my guitars, and as I did the tears finally came, just rolling down my face. I didn't know what to with the pieces, so I took them with me to the closet the intruder had hidden in.

The first thing I noticed when I opened the door was a strong scent of cologne. I counted myself lucky that I only had a few articles of clothing hanging in there. I'd have to air them out.

I put the pieces down on the floor, then looked in the back of the closet, where I had secreted the attaché case. It wasn't well hidden. The detectives would have found it if they had looked. The intruder either missed it or didn't have time to find it. If the latter was the case, then I walked in on him. Quite a coincidence that I'd arrived home just as he broke in when he could have done it any time while I was on stage at the Rum Boogie.

I carried the case to the kitchen table and set it there. I'd looked inside it at the storage unit, and then again when I brought it home. I decided to have another look before I did a better job of hiding it—or getting rid of it!

I popped the catches and opened it. It was still empty. There were several pockets in the lid, so I checked them, running my hands through them. The first time I did that, I'd come up empty, but this time I felt something with my fingertips. I reached down, snagged it and pulled it out.

It was a business card, and I recognized the name on it. Andrew Pac, Director of A&R, Starcade Records.

I MICROWAVED some old coffee that was left in the pot from that morning, sat at the kitchen table with the business card in the center of it. The case sat on the floor next to my chair. I hadn't yet decided what to do with it, but I knew I should decide because I'd tripped over it three times while getting the coffee.

The card intrigued me. I'd written Andy Pac off as someone who wasn't involved in the matter. Now I was having second thoughts. Maybe the case had belonged to Pac at one point. Or it may have been Corky's property—or Walter Rutlidge's—except why would either of them feel the need to carry one of Andy's business cards? Andy would carry some of his own cards in the case in order to give them out at events.

I touched the card with my forefinger. Corky had told me that he and Walter were the only ones who knew about the dropoff I'd made. But he was wrong, because Felix Nolan had known about it, and he could have told somebody else—or lots of somebody else's.

Like Andy Pac.

I WENT to sleep and woke about noon with a clearer idea in my head of what I had to do.

I had to check in with Chummy, see if he had managed to get anything from the book of numbers, but he really hadn't had it that long.

I had to talk to Corky and Walter again, talk to Andy Pac—and find someplace to hide that damned case because I tripped over the fucking thing again putting the coffee cup in the sink!

41

I WANTED TO SEE CORKY AND WALTER. IT WAS TIME TO see if they'd given me real numbers, or were just trying to placate me at the time.

I decided to call Walter. I hated to admit that I was still somewhat intimidated by Corky, the Major Country Music Producer. I used my landline to call him.

"Walter, it's Auggie."

"Hey, Auggie," Walter said. "Do you have good news?"

"I guess that depends on your definition of good news," I said. "I need to see the both of you."

"Yes, well, it's Saturday—"

"So you're not at Starcade," I said. "Where are you, on a golf course? I'll come there."

"Well, uh—"

"This is your problem I'm working on, Walter, not mine."

"You have a point," Walter said. "We're at the Ryman, planning some logistics for the Americana Honors night next week. We'll be here for the next hour if you want to come now. It's locked up, but I'll tell security to let you in."

"I'll be there in about fifteen minutes," I said.

THE RYMAN AUDITORIUM was the home of the Grand
Ole Opry from 1943 to 1974. Most of the major stars of the
past and present—from Hank Williams to Johnny Cash,
from Dolly Parton to Carrie Underwood—performed
there, causing it to be known as the "Carnegie Hall of
the South."

I had to pound on the door to get a security guard's
attention, only to find he wasn't the guard who had been
given my name. He eventually found the right one and let
me in.

"Mr. Barnes is in the auditorium," he told me.

I had been on the stage of the Ryman a couple of
times, but I never fail to catch my breath when I walk
through those doors into the auditorium itself. Just
thinking about the stars who had performed there was
intimidating. And being on the stage, looking out at the
crowd in the circular balcony, was almost a spiritual experience. Behind the crowds, the windows were shaped like
church windows, with clear and orange panes of glass
giving them a stained glass effect.

Here's where I have to say that, even though I haven't
released my own CD's, and even though I haven't head-
lined at the Ryman, just being on the stage makes me, to
some extent, a success. At least, that's what Elton
would say.

Down toward the front, about five rows back I saw
Corky, wearing his big black hat, Walter and a few other
people—two men along with a woman who was holding a
clipboard.

I walked down the aisle, and when I came within

earshot, Corky was saying he didn't want one of his artists sitting near another.

". . . but don't seat them too far apart. If they want to get into a hair-pulling match on TV, who are we to stop 'em?"

The woman seemed exasperated.

"Mr. Barnes, I have to be able to do my job—"

Corky saw me at that moment and shouted, "Auggie, my boy! Good to see you, hoss. Excuse me, folks. I have some business with this young fella. Walter?"

Corky came toward me, Walter running behind. When he reached me, the record mogul said, "Let's get away from these pains in the ass. They're tryin' to tell *me* where I can seat my people. Imagine that?"

He was waiting for an answer, so I said, "I can't."

"Damn right, you cain't! Now tell me, boy, what kind of good news you got for me? And boy, where did you get that bump on your head?"

I touched my forehead and said, "Compliments of some asshole who broke into my place and destroyed all my guitars."

"All of them?" Walter asked.

"Except for the Fender I had with me."

"A burglar?" Corky asked. "That's too damn bad."

"Burglar, my ass," I said. "This has to do with your shit, Corky, and I don't appreciate being kept in the dark. I want to know what you got me into? What was in that fucking attaché case that made somebody kill Felix Nolan, break into my place, destroy my property and knock me on the head?"

"Shh, boy," Corky said, looking around, "not so loud. Did you call the police about this break-in?"

"You bet I did. I've got to make an insurance claim for

my property. Those guitars were worth a lot of money. Hell, I should make you pay for them!"

Corky put his hands out, as if to push me, and said, "Let's take this outside."

We left the auditorium stopping just outside the doors.

"First off, boy," Corky said, "you got no proof that break-in had anything to do with our business. Second—"

"I'm gonna stop you right there, Corky," I said. "You're pissing me off by trying to talk your way out of this. Why don't we just agree that you've stuck me in the shit, hoping I wouldn't notice the smell? Well, guess what? It smells like shit!"

I had Andy Pac's business card in my pocket, the one I'd found in the case. I almost reached for it but thought better of it. Better to keep that little tidbit to myself. I was going to be talking to Andy, anyway.

"What did you tell the cops?" Corky asked.

"Well, two uniformed cops came and took a report so I could make an insurance claim. They weren't interested beyond that."

"That's good—"

"—but the detectives who showed up half-an-hour later wanted a little more information."

"Did you tell them—" Walter started.

"Did I tell them what, Walter? I don't know anything. But I'm the one getting fucked!"

"Nobody's fuckin' you, boy," Corky said. "You're gonna be taken care of. I'll replace your precious guitars, okay? But you've gotta keep workin' for me on this."

"Corky," I said, "I'm done unless you tell me what I'm looking for."

Corky glanced at Walter and said, "Shit."

42

CORKY GRABBED MY ARM AND WALKED ME UNTIL WE found an isolated corner, where he was sure we wouldn't be overheard, Walter followed helplessly.

"Now look, boy," Corky said, "this cain't get out, you hear? Nobody gets to know this. Not even the cops."

"As long as I get to know, I'm satisfied," I said, pointedly not making any promises. If I had to tell the cops to save my own skin, so be it.

Now, for the first time since I'd met him, Corky lowered his voice.

"Patsy Cline," he said, then looked around quickly to see if anyone had heard. Walter gave him an encouraging nod.

"In nineteen fifty-five Patsy signed a deal with Four Star records. She stayed with them until nineteen sixty, and then she signed with Decca, where she made her name."

"So?"

"So she recorded an album in nineteen fifty-four." He said very low.

I leaned into him. "No, she didn't."

"Oh yeah, she did. I found out about it, and I found the masters."

I stared at him, then looked at Walter, who nodded.

"That's what was in the attaché case?"

Corky nodded.

"Wait a minute," I said, "you found an unreleased Patsy Cline album and you gave it to Felix Nolan?"

"You gave it to him, technically," Corky said, "but yeah. Then he got himself killed, and they disappeared. That's what you're lookin' for now."

"Corky, would that would be worth a fortune—and a man's life?" I asked.

Corky looked at Walter.

"Wait a minute," I said. "There's still something you're not telling me."

They exchanged another glance.

"Corky—"

"Relax, Walter," Corky said. "He deserves to know, I guess."

"Know what?"

"There's another set of Masters."

Corky looked around, not wanting to be overheard. He lowered his voice even more.

"You can't repeat this to anyone, Auggie," he hissed. "Understand?"

"I understand."

"In nineteen sixty-two, Patsy met Elvis Presley at a St. Jude's charity event. They got along. She used to call everybody 'hoss.' Well, after she met Elvis, she started calling him 'Big Hoss.'"

I got a chill, but remained silent and listened.

"Apparently, sometime after that she and Elvis got

together and jammed. That's what's on this second set of masters."

"You've got a taped session of Elvis and Patsy Cline performing together?"

"Yes."

"But . . . what did they record."

"Some of his songs, some of hers."

"Wait a minute," I said. "Did you hear this recording yourself?"

"I did," Corky said, his eyes shining. "I actually heard Elvis sing 'Crazy.' And Patsy did 'Love Me Tender.' And they sang together on quite a few songs."

"Duets?" I said, in hushed tones. "Elvis and Patsy?"

Corky nodded.

"Corky," I said, "that would be worth a fortune."

"Don't I know it?" he asked, spreading his hands.

"Did you have them authenticated?" I asked.

"I didn't get a chance to," he said. "I listened to both sets myself. It sure sounded like Patsy on the early one, and Patsy and Elvis on the later one. But before we could authenticate them . . ."

"Then why did you have me give them away?"

"That ain't somethin' you need to know."

"Corky . . ."

"Yeah, yeah, okay," Corky said. "I was bein' black-mailed, and the scoundrel didn't ask for money, he asked for the masters."

"He knew about them?"

"Apparently," Walter said, with more than a hint of sarcasm.

"How?"

"We don't know," Corky said, "but he did."

"And you agreed to give them to him?"

"I did, but . . ." he hesitated.

"You made copies."

He nodded. "But we gave him the originals. We need to get them back before somebody else finds them."

"Can you use the copies to authenticate the recordings?"

"No."

"Wait," I said, "there's still something here I'm not getting. Where did you get the masters in the first place?"

"I bought 'em."

"From who?"

"I don't know," he said. "I bought them from a middleman."

"A go-between? Why didn't he just keep them and make himself a fortune?"

Corky shrugged and said, "Maybe he didn't know what to do with 'em. I do."

"Who was the go-between, Corky."

The big man hesitated.

"Come on, Corky. I'm getting tired of pulling things out of you."

Corky looked at Walter, who shrugged, leaving it up to him.

"Felix Nolan."

"But I gave the masters *back* to Felix Nolan."

"Right."

"So the man you bought them from blackmailed you to get them back?"

"Yes."

"Why would he do that?"

"He gets the masters and Corky's money," Walter said.

"And you don't know who Nolan got the masters from?"

"No," Corky said.

"Or what he intended to do with them?"

"No."

"Well," I reasoned, "maybe he was making a deal with somebody and that's who killed him."

"Or," Walter said, "maybe somebody else he was blackmailing."

"Do the cops know about the blackmail?" I asked Corky.

"No."

"If they do," Walter said, "Corky will end up the number one suspect."

"And get me off the hook."

"Whoa, Auggie, boy," Corky said, "that kind of scandal could kill me in this business. What help would I be to anyone then? How could I help you?"

Did he have any intention of helping me? I didn't know. Could I throw him to the cops to save myself? Probably . . . But maybe not yet.

"Okay," I said, "not a word from me, for now."

"Thank you, Auggie, thanks," Corky said. He looked around again. "So now what? We still gotta find those masters."

"What about the money?" I asked. "How much did you pay?"

Corky hesitated again, then said, "A million bucks."

"A million?"

He waved it off. "I'll make back ten times that."

"If we find the masters," I said.

"That's your job."

I stared at the two of them, then stepped back, shaking my head.

"What's wrong?" Walter asked.

"This isn't right," I said.

"What ain't?" Corky asked.

"You guys hiring me to do this."

"Which part?" Walter asked.

"Any of it," I said. "First delivering the masters to Nolan, and then to find them again after he shows up dead. Why me? You could damn sure afford somebody who knows what they're doing. Walter, you've used lots of agencies before."

"Auggie," Walter said, "a reputable agency wouldn't have touched this—at least, not without asking Corky what he was being blackmailed for."

"There, see?" I said, pointing at them. "I didn't even ask that. Maybe I don't know what I'm doing."

"Somebody broke into your place," Walter said. "You must be getting close, else why would they warn you off that way."

"That could've been a simple burglary that I walked in on."

"You know that's not true," Walter said. "Why would he smash your guitars?"

"Because he was pissed that there wasn't anything of value to steal."

"He could have taken your guitars and sold them," Walter said. "No, no coincidence here, Auggie. You're getting close."

"You gotta find those masters," Corky said.

"You have copies. Why don't you just use those? Remaster them, digitize them."

"I need the originals to prove they're real before I can do anything with them."

"You paid a million bucks without knowing?"

"I was trusting my own ear," Corky said. "It was worth it to me."

"What about a safety copy?" I asked. Masters were usually stored in a cold place, and the safety copy was a backup.

"Hopefully," Corky said, "there ain't one. I wanna have the only copy."

I stared at them and said slowly, "An unpublished Patsy Cline album, that's something, but Patsy and Elvis together?"

"Yup," Corky said.

The musician in me had to ask, "Are you sure it's her?"

"I'm positive," Corky said.

"How is it?"

"Not that it matters," Corky said, "but it's pretty dang bad."

"And her and Elvis?"

"Rough," he said, "but hell, if it's really them . . ."

"Are the masters marked? Labeled?" I asked.

"The first one just says Patsy nineteen-fifty-four," Corky said.

"And the other one?"

Corky grinned.

"Somebody wrote on it 'The Honky Tonk Big Hoss Boogie.' Ain't that a kick?"

43

I LEFT THE RYMAN, STILL IN THE SHIT. BUT AT LEAST now I knew where it was coming from. It still stank like hell, but I had the feeling Corky and Walter had told me everything—except Corky's big secret, and I didn't really think I needed to know that. I didn't *want* to know.

When I got outside, I stood there transfixed for a moment by indecision. What should I do next?

I had on a pocket T that day, with George Harrison across the front. "While My Guitar Gently Weeps" is still one of my favorite songs. I put my hand in the pocket and came out with Andy Pac's card. I needed to talk to him again, but first I thought I'd go back to Felix Nolan's place in Germantown and have another look around. Maybe I'd missed something that connected him to Pac because I didn't know what I was looking for the first time.

I put the card away and went to my car.

THERE WAS loud music coming from the neighbor's apartment again. But it had so much bass I couldn't tell what the hell it was. Volume and bass were a great way to kill a melody, especially in a confined space. I guessed that neighbor Melanie—Melanie? Yeah, that was it—didn't know that.

I went to Nolan's door, got out my picks and let myself in. While I was there the music in Melanie's apartment stopped. I paused, to see if she'd leave, but I didn't hear her door open. Returning to my search, it was soon pretty evident there was nothing in the place that would lead me to Andy Pac.

But there was something that bothered me — no odor of cologne in the place. For somebody who reeked of it that night when I gave him the case, you'd think there'd be something in the air. I went back to his bathroom and looked for his cologne, but didn't find any. That puzzled me.

I left the apartment, closing and locking the door behind me, still wondering about the cologne, which I'd smelled that night on the bridge, and then again in my apartment in the closet. It didn't make sense to me. I had to try and work it out—

The door to Melanie's apartment opened.

"Hey!" she said, "ya'll came back."

"Hey," I said back. "Melanie, right?"

"You remembered," she said. "You're . . ."

"Auggie."

"Right, right." She had on cut-off jeans and a tight-fitting top with tiny straps, showing a lot of skin as well as the outline of large nipples. She had good legs, and her feet were bare. They were a little dirty and the nails retained the remnants of some purple polish. The overall effect was kind of sexy/slutty. "What brings you back here?"

"I just have a few questions for you . . . if it's okay?"

"Sure, why not? Come on in."

I entered the apartment, but even before I did, I caught the smell in the air. Weed. There was also someone else there; a guy fast asleep on the couch.

"Don't mind him," she said. "He lives upstairs. I brought him in to fuck me, but after a few tokes, he fell asleep. Useless."

"Too bad."

She turned to me like she just had a bright idea.

"How about you?"

"How about me . . . what?"

"Wanna fuck?"

"Look, Melanie—"

"Or, if ya'll are afraid of catchin' a disease or somethin' I could suck your dick . . . or you could fuck my tits!" She grabbed the bottom of her shirt and pulled it up, revealing acres of smooth skin, bottom heavy breasts and dark brown nipples.

"Look, Melanie, they're pretty nice tits, but—"

Suddenly, she looked down at herself sadly.

"Yeah, well, they used to be nice," she said, pulling the shirt back down. "Ain't that a bitch? A woman gets older, starts to sag here and there, but if all you young studs would give us a chance you'd see we're better in bed than we ever were. It's all about experience."

I recalled my own experience on the road with the cougar and knew she was right. But that combined with my night with Allegra, and I wasn't exactly starving for sex. Of course, if the guy hadn't been there, and I *was* . . .

"Okay," she said, grabbing a half-full beer bottle from the coffee table in front of the sleeping guy, "you said you had some questions?" She held the longneck the way women did, by the neck.

"Your neighbor, Felix," I said. "You said he had lots of visitors."

"Visitors, customers," she said, "whatever you wanna call 'em."

"Customers?"

"Hey, you got any weed?" she suddenly asked. "We just finished my last, and Felix was my connection. I need-a find somebody new."

"Wait a minute," I said, "he dealt drugs out of his apartment?"

"Yeah, nobody ever said he was a whatayallit, rock scientist."

"Rocket," I corrected.

"What?"

"Never mind. Look, did he ever get any visits from an Asian guy?"

"Asians, blacks, Polacks, he was an equal opportunity drug dealer."

"Lots of Asians?" I asked.

"Well, I only remember one. Saw him a coupla times, guy with thick glasses with black rims. Kinda nerdy lookin'."

Could have been anybody, but sure sounded like Andy Pac. Maybe I had my connection.

"Okay, Melanie, thanks."

"That's it? No more questions?"

"Nope."

"How about a quick handjob before ya'll go?" she asked. "Only ten bucks?"

"That's okay," I said. "I'm good—but look." I took out a twenty and handed it to her. "Thanks for your help."

"Sure, lover," she said, tucking the twenty into her jean

pocket. They were skin tight, but she managed to squeeze it in.

"I could use a hand job," the guy on the sofa said, looking around blearily.

"Hey, you better go," she said. "I gotta make use of him while he's awake."

"Good luck."

"Just between you and me," she said, "he likes to fuck me in the butt so he can pretend I'm a guy, but what the hell, a poke is a poke, right?"

"Whatever gets you off," I said, and got out of there.

44

OKAY, THE WHOLE THING ABOUT THE COLOGNE BUGGED me. I drove from Germantown to Harley's house. I wanted to see how he was, and maybe bounce some stuff off of him. I just hoped I wouldn't find him in the same condition as last time.

When I got there, I was encouraged to find the front door had been fixed. Harley must have made the call on that.

I rang the bell, then tried the door. It was open and I went in.

"What the hell are ya ringin' the bell for?" Harley shouted from the sofa. "Don't ya know I got ass cancer?"

"What if I was the Avon Lady?" I asked.

"She'd have to go someplace else, 'cause she ain't gettin' no action here. How you doin', boy?"

"Checking on you, old man."

He had a few beer bottles on the table in front of him, the remnants of a bag of pork rinds, and a coffee cup with some brown crud at the bottom.

"I'm still alive if that's what yer worried about," Harley said. "Get me a beer and pull up a chair. Oh, and get one for yerself."

I went to the kitchen. The sink was empty, but take-out bags and boxes were overflowing from the garbage. I got two Rolling Rocks from the frig and carried them back to the living room and handed Harley one. That close I could smell his body odor—sweat and cancer.

Harley chugged half the beer, then lit a cigarette.

"You supposed to be doin' that?" I asked.

"What?"

"Smoking and drinking."

"What's the difference? I'm dyin', ain't I? Might as well enjoy myself. Speakin' of that, bring hotdogs next time you come, will ya?"

"Judging from all the take-out boxes in the kitchen you ain't missing many meals."

"The one bright spot about dyin' is it don't matter what you drink or eat, anymore. And they's lot of food you can have delivered."

No, I thought, not if you embrace death and have decided not to fight. I always thought if I ever got cancer that I wouldn't do chemo. It kills you to save you. Looking at Harley, I thought, well, yeah, okay, at his age, but what if I contracted it at my age?

"What's up, kiddo?"

"I thought if you had nothin' better to do I'd bounce some shit off you."

"Still workin' that case?"

"Yeah," I said, "I found out some stuff."

He started to cough, and I waited until it had run its course.

"Okay, shoot," he growled.

I told him what had happened after I got back from Memphis, everything I knew, everything I surmised, and then everything I learned from talking to Corky.

"Patsy Cline?" he asked, excitedly. Harley was a big fan. "Now there was a singer! And the King? Goddamn! He says it was bad?"

"Well, it was her first," I said. "There must've been a reason it was never released. And the other thing . . . Well, it doesn't really matter if it was good or bad . . . if it was them."

"Yeah, you said it. But shit, could Patsy do anythin' bad?"

"Didn't have to be her—or them—that was bad, it could've been the quality of the recording," I offered.

"Hey, yeah," he said, grabbing the bone I'd thrown him. "You're right."

Then I told him about going back to Felix Nolan's apartment, and what I found out from Melanie when she wasn't flashing her tits at me.

Harley chuckled. "I remember days like that; women throwin' themselves atcha because yer a private dick. Get it?"

"I get it, Harley," I said, "but I don't get it. This thing with the cologne is really buggin' me."

"Just take a deep breath, relax and tell me what yer thinkin'," Harley said.

"I'll tell you what I'm thinkin'," I said. "Not smelling any cologne in Nolan's apartment, I'm startin' to wonder if that's really his body in the morgue."

"Believe me," Harley said, "they made sure that was Nolan's body, probably from his fingerprints."

"Damn it, you're right."

"I'm thinkin' *you're* thinkin' about this the wrong way."

"What do you mean?"

"I mean," Harley said, "what you should be thinkin' is, was that Felix Nolan on the bridge who you gave the case to?"

PART 4

"Sober ain't all it's cracked up to be."

Music by Augusto Velez-Colon
Lyrics by Harley Rayborn

45

Damn it, but he was right.

Shaking my head, I realized that even cancer-riddled, Harley had a mind like a steel trap.

That was *not* Felix Nolan on the bridge, smelling of cologne. Nolan was no doubt already dead at that point. It *was* the same guy in my closet, though, smelling of the same cologne.

Now, where else had I smelled it? That was driving me crazy.

"Based on this premise," Harley told me, "you've got some new moves to make."

Looking at him, I knew he wanted me to get what those moves were, and didn't want me to have to ask.

"Yes, I do," I said. "I'll check on you again, later."

"And bring hotdogs!" he yelled as I went out.

In my car, driving back towards downtown, I was wondering, What are those new moves?

———

I NOW KNEW what I was looking for. Early masters would be on reel-to-reel tapes. They would have to be stored somewhere cool. Somewhere climate controlled, which Felix Nolan's storage unit was not.

But a safe depository in a bank was. According to his bank statement, Nolan had such a box, but we had now established that it wasn't Felix Nolan I had handed the attaché case to, so why would the masters be in his box at the bank?

No, I wasn't going to find those tapes until I discovered who I had handed them to. And the chances were pretty good that he also killed Nolan so that he would be able to meet me and accept the case.

It was flimsy, but it was all I had. Where had I smelled that cologne before?

And on who?

WHEN I GOT HOME I used my cell to call Allegra.

"How are you?" she asked. "Is everything all right?"

"That depends on what you mean by everything."

"Do the police have any idea who broke into your place and trashed your guitars?"

"No," I said. "That reminds me, I have to take care of my insurance claim. I better do that today. Are you all right?"

"I'm fine," she said. "I enjoyed the ride to Beale Street. I'm just sorry the night didn't end with us in your bed."

"Me, too," I said, wholeheartedly. "We'll have to do something to remedy that."

"When?"

"I'll have to call you," I said. "I've still got some work

to do on this, and the insurance claim. I'll need that money to replace my axes."

"Will you be able to?" she asked.

"No," I said, "not the sentiment behind some of them, but it's my business, and I need to have more than one. I'll just have to buy a few that have no sentimental value to me."

"Well," she said, "call me when you get time in your schedule."

"I will," I said. "I also have to go out and smell some colognes."

"What?"

"I smelled cologne last night when I got hit by that door," I said. "And I also smelled it the night I was on the bridge."

"So it was the same person?"

"Unless two people wear that same suffocating shit scent."

"It was that bad?"

"Yes, and I've smelled it one more place. Probably wasn't as bad, but I just can't remember when. I will, though."

"Well, good luck," she said. "I'll talk to you soon."

"Yes, you will," I assured her, and hung up.

I HUNG a guitar around my neck—it was when I was the most comfortable, and the way I did most of my songwriting. In this instance, though, I wanted to see if it would calm me enough to enable me to think.

All I had left was my Fender, so I walked around with it, fingering some chords from time to time, or simply plucking out a melody. I wondered if Detective Hollinger knew what I now knew, that the man on the bridge wasn't Felix Nolan? Was that something I should tell him? If I did, he'd wonder how I knew. He'd want proof, and I didn't have any. So probably my best next move was to go out and find some.

I microwaved a can of chili—a late lunch, or an early dinner—ate it from a bowl while I continued to walk around, still with the Fender around my neck. I was standing in front of the window, having just finished the last spoonful, listening to the music drifting up from the street, when my cell phone rang.

"Auggie?"

"Yeah?"

"It's Chummy."

"Hey, Chummy. What—"

"Ya gotta meet me, kid," he said, cutting me off. "Ya gotta meet me now."

"What for, Chummy?"

"I got somethin' for ya, on that book."

"The code?" I asked. I put the empty bowl down. "You broke Nolan's code?"

"Not me," he said, "but I can take you to somebody who did."

"Who?"

"Just meet me," Chummy said, "and you can ask all the questions you want."

"Okay," I said, taking the guitar from around my neck and setting it aside gently, "where?"

46

It was dusk when I pulled up in front of Chummy's place. He came right out and got in the car.

"Okay, kid, go!" he said.

"You haven't told me yet where."

"Shelby Park."

"What part?"

"Front of the Nature Center."

"It's closed now, you know."

"I know. The person we're meeting picked the location."

"And this is the person who broke Nolan's code?" I asked.

"This is the person who says they have somethin' for you from the book," Chummy said. "Why don't we talk while we drive?"

"Are we on a time limit?"

"Yes, we are."

I put the car in drive and floored it.

. . .

SHELBY BOTTOMS NATURE CENTER was over eight hundred acres of wetlands and trails along the Cumberland. A major tourist attraction, it was closed and dark when we pulled up in front of the main entrance.

"Park down the street," Chummy said. "We'll walk back."

"How are we supposed to get inside?" I asked. "You going to pick this lock, too?"

"It'll be taken care of for us," he said.

"By who?"

"Just drive on and park."

I did as he asked, but when I turned off the motor, I turned to face him.

"I'm not going any further until you tell me what's going on."

"Look," he said, "I told you I did a job a few years back for somebody. Because of that, they owe me."

"And you called this favor in for me? You hardly know me, Chummy."

"You're Harley's boy," he said, "and you needed somebody who could figure out a code. Believe me, that's this person. But there are conditions."

"What conditions?"

"Once we get out of the car," Chummy said, "you can't ask any more questions unless it has to do with the book."

"That's it?"

"That's it."

"What is this, top secret?"

He looked me in the eye and said, "Yes."

I stared at him for a few seconds, then said, "Now, wait a minute. Are you telling me—"

"All I'm tellin' you is that there's somebody who has some answers for you. Do you wanna talk to 'em?"

"Yes," I said.

"Okay," he said, opening his door. "Let's go."

We got out of the car and walked to the main entrance of the Nature Center.

"How do we get in?" I asked.

Chummy put his hand on the front door and pushed. It opened.

I said, "Let's go."

"I can't," Chummy said. "You have to go in alone."

"Why?"

"That's how it's supposed to go down."

"Well . . . where do I go?"

"Walk straight across, take the trail that's marked."

"I have to walk on one of the trails?"

"Yes."

"For how long?"

"Until you're contacted."

"Chummy, come on," I said, "all this cloak-and-dagger stuff—"

He held his hand up to silence me.

"You don't have to go in, you know."

"All right," I said. "Where's the book?" I put my hand out.

"It's on the trail."

"So I *do* have to go in I want the book back."

He shrugged.

"Great. Where will you be?"

"Out here."

"Okay."

I opened the door and went inside. It was dark, but after a few moments my eyes adjusted and I was able to see my way around. I crossed the floor without bumping into anything, came to a place where the trails started.

There was a red cloth tied to one of the turnstiles. I jumped it and went outside onto the trail.

There was still some light for me to see by, but there was nothing to see but the trees and bushes and trail — no man with my book. I wondered if Chummy was just trying to make me think this guy was some sort of spy, or if he really was? C.I.A. maybe? Or an ex-spy? Jesus, this was way more than I bargained for.

"Stop."

At first, I wasn't sure I heard right, but I stopped and listened.

"You alone?" a voice asked.

"Yeah, I'm alone."

"Where's Chummy?"

"Outside."

I looked around, didn't see anybody. Then, suddenly, a figure stepped out from the cover of a brush. It was dark enough for his face to be hidden. He was wearing jeans and a jean jacket. I got the impression of long hair.

"You Auggie?" he asked.

"I'm Auggie."

"I'm Chummy's friend."

"I figured," I said. "So we exchange some kind of secret greeting or handshake?"

"You think that's funny?" the man asked.

"Kinda," I said. "I guess not. You want to tell me what this is all about?"

He was about twenty feet away from me, far enough that I was still unable to make out his face clearly in the dark.

"Seems to me you know more about that than I do," the man said. "Chummy called me and said he needed help with some kind of code for you." He took the book from his jacket pocket. "A code in here."

"And you're an expert on codes?"

"I am."

"How did you come by that talent?"

"That's not a question I'm inclined to answer. You want to know what's in this book, or not?"

"Why are you doing this?" I asked.

"Because Chummy's good people," he said, "and he asked me to."

"And I guess it does me no good to ask your name?"

"It would do you no good to know my name, Auggie," he said. "Just call me . . . Cal."

"And I guess there's no point in me asking if we can do this somewhere else, Cal?"

"I have my reasons for meeting you here," the man said. "Now can we get on with it, because I got more reasons for not wanting to be here too much longer."

"Okay," I said, giving up. "Let me have it."

"Whoever this book belonged to," he said, "was black-mailing a lot of people."

"Blackmail?"

He nodded. "That's right."

"Blackmailing them for what?"

"Well, now, that's not written down in here," he said. "But what *is* in here are a whole lot of names and a whole lot of numbers."

"Dollars?"

"You bet."

"Is there any way for me to be able to read it?"

"Sure." He took another notebook from his pocket. "I wrote it all down in here for you."

"That's great!" I started toward him and he held his hands out, a book in each.

"No, no," he said. "Don't come any closer. I'm gonna lay these down on the ground here. When I'm gone, you can pick them up."

He crouched and set them both down on the ground, then stood up.

"I don't suppose you want to know how I broke the code?" he asked. "Or what kind of code it was? It was pretty simple, really. It's based on a principle of first and last—"

"No, you're right," I said, cutting him off.

"About what?"

"I don't want to know. I appreciate your help, though."

"I did it for Chummy," Cal said. "Thank him. Now, you give me about ten minutes to get out of here, and then go back the way you came."

"You got it," I said. "Thanks, Cal. Maybe next time we'll have a beer."

"That sounds right, Auggie. Adios." He disappeared into the brush.

Adios?

CHUMMY LOOKED surprised when I came back.

"That fast?"

"That's it."

"What happened?"

"He broke the code," I said, "wrote it all down for me in another book."

"Then that should be helpful to you, shouldn't it?"

"Yeah, it should. He's kind of odd, your friend, Cal."

"Yeah, he is."

I frowned and said, "When he left he said 'adios.'"

Chummy laughed and said, "Yeah, he does that."

47

I drove Chummy to his house, and then went back to my place. I sat at the table with both books, Nolan's and Cal's, which held the translation. I turned page after page, reading the names of Felix Nolan's blackmail victims, and the amounts he was receiving from each. They weren't well-known names—not to me, anyway. In fact, I didn't recognize any of them.

Nolan had himself a nice little cottage industry. He remained at home and collected weekly or monthly sums from the people in the book. How he got himself set up this way I didn't have a clue. Where had he gotten his information from? How did he know the secrets of twenty-two men and women?

Twenty-two. Sixteen men and six women. And they were now all suspects in the death of Felix Nolan. Did the cops know about them? I doubted it since I had the book. That meant that while I was looking at twenty-two suspects, the cops may have still only been looking at one—me.

I was about to do some math when I turned to the last

page and saw that Cal had done it for me. He'd added up the sums of money each person paid per month. Felix Nolan was collecting about forty thousand dollars a month. Less than two thousand dollars a person. He wasn't a greedy man, probably figured out what each person could afford, and had only asked for that much. His victims chose to make the payments rather than go to the police. Maybe they had even included Nolan in their budget. This much for groceries, this much for utilities, this much for blackmail.

And then I realized something. I leafed through the book again, but I came to the same realization. Corky's name wasn't in there. Nolan apparently hadn't been bleeding Corky monthly. He got his money from Corky all at one time. Then whoever had killed him had stolen the tapes. For what purpose, if not to sell them back to Corky?

I set both books in the center of the table and stared at them. I was hungry but didn't want to go out again. There was some frozen fried chicken in my freezer, so I microwaved it, ate it at the table and washed it down with beer while considering my predicament.

I had twenty-two names, but no addresses. I would probably be able to find out who some of these people were, where they lived, what they did for a living, by doing a Google search on my laptop, but what then? Go to each of them and ask if they had killed Felix Nolan? Would the guilty party say yes?

I could probably get myself out of Detective Hollinger's crosshairs by handing the book over to him. Could I do that without getting myself into trouble? Wouldn't he want to know where I got it, how, and why I'd kept it this long? Maybe I should mail it, or messenger it to him. At least that way he'd have it, and might start looking away from me.

Or maybe I should just man up, meet with him and give it to him. He might even be impressed with me, that I had found something he and his men had missed.

I checked the time. Close to midnight. I'd been sitting there for hours. It was too late to call Hollinger. I'd leave that for the morning.

I put the two books in the attaché case, which I still hid in the closet. Then I sat up till two, making a list of the damage that had been done to my axes. In the morning I'd call Mutual America before I called Detective Hollinger.

I'd need to get a check from the insurance company as soon as possible. I had sessions coming up, plus some gigs, including the upcoming Americana Honors and the CMA's.

I turned in, then. There was a lot to do tomorrow. Hopefully, by the end of it, I'd have more of an idea of how my life was going to play out.

48

IN THE MORNING I HAD AN ENGLISH MUFFIN, SOME fruit, and coffee for breakfast then called my insurance guy. While we were on the phone, he had me log onto his company's website, and he walked me through making my claim online. He assured me a check would be cut asap. I was shocked at how simple it was. I thanked him and promised him two tickets to the CMA's. I hoped I'd be able to deliver.

After that, I called Allegra on her cell. She said she was at work at a temp job, but took the call.

"Wait," she said. I waited. When she came back on she said, "All right, I'm outside. What's up?"

"I just wanted to let you know . . . I don't know how much I'll be around the next few days."

"Why's that?"

"I'm going to do something that may or may not be smart. If it's smart, we can have dinner tonight. If it's not . . ."

"Auggie, what are you gonna do?"

I told her about calling Hollinger and giving him the book.

"You'll have to tell him where you got it," she said. "And how."

"I know."

"You think he'll let you go? Or lock you up?"

"I'm hoping for the first, but preparing for the second."

"By calling me?"

"I just wanted you to know, if you don't hear from me for a while, it isn't because . . . well, you know."

"That you're a real prick, like other men?"

"Right."

She laughed. "I wouldn't have thought that."

"Thanks."

"What does your friend say about this?"

"Harley? I haven't told him."

"Don't you think you should?" she asked. "He might have a better idea."

"Well, I thought I'd better figure this one out myself," I said, "but maybe you're right."

"He's sick," she said. "It'll take his mind off how sick he is if you talk to him."

She was right, of course. It would be good for Harley, and probably better for me to get either his blessing or a better idea.

I CALLED Harley and he told me to come right over. I asked if he needed anything and he said Chummy had brought him some stuff. He sounded good, stronger than I'd heard him lately.

When I pulled up in front of the house, Harley was

sitting on the porch. That was a good sign. When I got to the steps, I saw he was holding a glass and smoking a cigar.

"Is that booze?"

"Yeah."

"You supposed to be drinking that?"

"Why? You afraid it's gonna kill me?"

"But I thought you quit."

"Kid," he said, "sober ain't what it's all cracked up to be."

"Holy shit," I said. "What a line. Can I steal that for a song?"

"Be my guest."

"You got any more of that?"

"Don't drink my booze, Auggie," he said. "It's good booze and you usually don't drink hard liquor. It'll be wasted on you. Get a beer from the frig."

"I'll be right back."

I went in the front door and walked to the kitchen. In passing, I saw what a mess the living room was. I thought maybe I should send a cleaner over. I'd check with Harley, make sure it was all right.

On the way with a Leinie in my hand, I saw his laptop. It was on the dining room table, the lid closed and covered with a layer of dust. I knew that Harley only used it for emails. He hated the Internet.

I joined him outside and sat next to him. He had two good, sturdy wooden lounge chairs with no cushions. Didn't he need a cushion?

"How are you feeling?"

"Actually, a lot better," Harley said. He sipped his drink. I knew it was good Scotch. There were no ice cubes in it. Then he put the cigar to his mouth and drew then blew luxuriously. "Yeah, a lot better. I think the booze and cigars are helping."

"Alternative medicine."

"Yeah, maybe. How's your case goin'?"

"That's why I'm here," I said. "I'm getting ready to talk to the cops and give them what I've got, but I wanted to bounce some stuff off you first."

"Okay, so bounce."

I told him about Chummy's buddy, Cal, translating the book for me, told him I was considering giving the cops the books, and the information about the safety deposit box.

"Don't fool yourself," he said. "They know about the box. But if you give them the books, you'll have to tell how you got them. That's breaking-and-entering and with-holding evidence."

"I thought maybe Hollinger would just take them and be glad."

"Be smart, kid," he said. "Don't trust a cop to do the right thing."

"Then what do I do? Mail the books to him?"

"No," Harley said, turning his head and looking at me, "solve the case yourself. Find the stuff, find the killer, give it all to the cops. Then they'll be too happy to prosecute you."

"Look, Hollinger seems like a right guy—"

"He's not a right guy or a nice guy, Auggie," Harley said.

"Do you know him?"

"No, but I know cops."

He poured some more Scotch from the bottle that was sitting on his right. I hadn't seen it before. It was 24-year-old Highland Park.

"Tell me more about the book."

I told him about all the names, and the amounts, and the fact that Corky's name wasn't there.

"Wow," he said, "a very businesslike blackmailer, and not too greedy. Bleeding just enough from each person so that they'd be able to afford it. Smart."

"But then Corky came along, and he was the brass ring."

"And going for it got him killed."

"Yeah, maybe," I said. "What are you thinking about?"

"The names in the book," he said. "Did you check them out? On the computer?"

"No," I said. "I thought looking at them as suspects would make it all harder. Corky's the big fish."

"So you think he killed Nolan?"

"Or had him killed," I said. "And then maybe the killer decided to cash in and kept the tapes for himself."

"That's a thought."

"And then there's Andy Pac," I said. "If I'm still going to do this myself, I need to talk to him again."

Harley looked at the end of his cigar.

"Why don't we check the names, just for fun?" he asked.

"Now?"

"Sure, why not? You got something better to do?"

He looked at me. His eyes seemed clearer than they had the last couple of times I'd seen him. Maybe this would be good for him.

"Is your laptop working?" I asked.

"I suppose. I ain't used it in a while."

"Okay," I said, getting up, "so let's see."

49

I brought the laptop out to the porch so Harley wouldn't have to move. He could drink his Scotch, smoke his cigar and watch me surf.

He watched intently as I Googled the names one-by-one, bringing up as much information on each of them as I could. But after we'd gone through eleven names, he stopped me.

"I think that's it," he said.

"What do you mean?"

"Well, look at what we have," he said. "In one way or another, each of these first eleven people is involved in the music world. DJs, producers, engineers, PR people . . . what does that tell you?"

I thought a moment, then said, "Somebody in the business was giving this information to Felix Nolan."

"That's the only conclusion I can see."

"But why would that person pass the information on and not act on it himself?"

"Maybe he's just a gossip," Harley said. "Maybe he has the balls to gossip, but not to actually blackmail people."

"Until now," I said. "Until the Patsy Cline and Elvis tapes."

"The brass ring," Harley said. "This one he couldn't pass up."

"So it's somebody in the business, who has access to people's secrets."

"Somebody who knows how to dig," Harley said.

"Publicity, public relations . . ."

". . . or somebody who's good with a computer."

"Or both."

I got up, went and got myself another beer, and came back. We sat and drank and thought for a while.

Then we looked at each other at the same moment.

"What's the guy's name you said you still have to—"

"Andy Pac," I said. "He's the guy. He's on the inside."

"But didn't Corky Barnes tell you nobody knew what was going on but him and his lawyer?"

"Yeah, he did."

"Well, Barnes wouldn't blackmail himself," Harley said. "What about the lawyer. What's his name?"

"Walter Rutlidge," I said.

"Yeah, him. Why wouldn't he grab for the brass ring?" Harley asked.

"They've been friends for years," I said. "They came into the business together."

"But Barnes is the top dog, right?"

"Right."

Harley shrugged and said, "Everybody wants to knock off the top dog."

"So," I said, thoughtfully, "instead of regarding these twenty-two people as suspects, I should be looking at Rutlidge and Pac."

"I think you're right about these folks," Harley said.

"The amount of blackmail fit right into their budget. That means the blackmailer—Nolan—was both smart and not greedy. Now that he's dead they'll find out they're off the hook, but none of them was payin' him enough money to get him killed."

"I get it." I logged off and closed his laptop, set it aside.

"Now let me explain somethin' to you," Harley said, "so you can't claim later I never told you this."

"What?"

"This is an active murder case," he said. "The cops don't like PIs who meddle in active cases. You could get into a lot of trouble."

"Are you telling me to do it, or not to do it?" I asked.

"Kid," Harley said, "I'm tellin' you not to get caught."

50

I GOT IN MY CAR AND TOOK OUT MY CELL PHONE.

"Walter?"

"Yes, Auggie?"

"That's right," I said. "Where's Andy Pac right now?"

"Pac? Why do you want him?"

"I've got some questions for him," I said. "In fact, I've got some for you, too, but I'm going to talk to Pac first."

"As far as I know he's in his office—although it is getting near lunch time."

It was close to one, and if I remembered correctly, Pac had gone to lunch at noon last time. So by one, he should be back.

"I'm coming over," I said. "Don't go anywhere, Walter."

"Well, I might—"

"Whatever you have to do, put it off," I said. "I've got some important questions."

"Well . . . all right."

"Make sure I don't have any trouble getting into the building."

I hung up. Did he sound nervous? Could it be that

Walter was looking to topple the big dog? Was he tired of playing second fiddle to Corky? Those were the questions.

I put my car in gear and headed for Music Row.

I PULLED over near the park, picked up my cell phone again. I called Allegra. I wanted her to take on Andy Pac.

"I'm sorry to bother you with this," I said when she picked up.

"Don't worry," she said. "What's up?"

"How much contact did you have with Andy Pac when you worked for Corky?"

"Andy? He stopped to talk to me whenever he came to see Corky."

"Talk to you how? Hit on you?"

"If he was hitting on me he was very inept at it. He was all smiles and compliments. But he never asked me out, or anything."

"What else?"

"Like what?"

"What kind of a guy was he?"

"Kind of nerdy," she said. "I was surprised that he did his job so well. A&R guys are usually a lot more gregarious then he was. I got the feeling that he did his job by flying under the radar. You know, going to a club to listen to a band, and not letting anyone know why he was there until he had some business to discuss. Other guys will go in, flash their credentials, get a meal and some drinks on the house, even a girl. Andy wasn't like that, but I don't think it was deliberate. You know, like a plan. I think that was the way he was."

"You ever hear him argue with Corky?"

"Oh, sure," she said. "Everybody argued with Corky. He gets under everybody's skin."

"Did you hear any specifics when they argued?"

"I just heard them yelling at each other in Corky's office," she said. "It was usually a difference of opinion about this artist or that one. But I don't have any specifics. It's not like I listened at the door or anything."

I believed her. She didn't strike me as the listening at the door type—although I wished, at that moment, that she was.

"Okay, Allegra. Thanks."

"Why all the questions about Andy?"

"I'll tell you when I see you."

"And when will that be?"

"I'll call you."

"That's what they all say," she said and hung up.

51

I WALKED TO THE STARCADE BUILDING, HAD NO TROUBLE entering—just had to tell the guard my name—checked the directory for Andy Pac's office, and then took the elevator. There was no secretary for me to get by, so I walked right into Pac's office. He looked up from his desk and hurriedly grabbed his glasses so he could see me clearly. He was wearing a shirt and tie; a sports jacket hung on the back of his chair.

"What do you want?"

"I have some questions."

"I wasn't very happy with your questions last time," Pac said.

"Then you're probably going to like them even less now."

"Look, I can call security—"

"Go ahead," I said. "I have your boss's okay to be here." That was only a partial lie since it was Walter Rutlidge's okay I actually had.

He frowned. "All right, ask your damn questions and then get out."

I remained standing at the door since I hadn't been invited to sit.

Andy Pac was the A&R guy at Starcade. A&R stood for "artists & repertoire," but many of us in the business said it stood for "attitude & rejection." You can't get into the record business without an A&R guy noticing you. They're pretty much the gatekeepers of the label they work for. I had known plenty of good guys working A&R over the years, but there are also those who used their jobs to benefit themselves first and then their labels. I'm talking greased palms and polished knobs. In Hollywood, they called it the casting couch.

Andy Pac appeared to be a myopic nerd, but I'd never done business with him. It's the people who keep low *and* keep their ears open who can come up with tasty tidbits that are blackmail worthy.

"Andy, I'm guessing you're good at your job?"

"I get the job done."

"Yeah, and you do it quietly, I bet," I said.

"What's that mean?"

"Means nobody knows you're around," I said. "You work for one of the biggest labels in Nashville, but yet nobody seems to have heard of you. Makes it easy to pick up things.

"Things? What things?"

"You know, things people don't want other people to know. Secrets. I'll bet you could blackmail a lot of people in this town if you wanted to."

Suddenly, Pac got uncomfortable.

"That—that's illegal."

"Yeah, it is, but you know, that never seems to stop blackmailers."

"Look," Pac said, "I've got work to do—"

"Your boss wants you to answer these questions," I said. "Do you want to do this in his office?"

"N-no," Pac said, "no, that's okay."

"Come to think of it," I said, "when Corky decided to hire me, how come you were left out of it? Why was it he and Walter Rutlidge who did the hiring?"

"I don't know," Pac said. "I don't know everything they do."

"But you know about the guy who got killed, right? Felix Nolan?"

"I—I never heard of him."

"Now he was a blackmailer," I said. "Had a book full of names. And you know what? All the name are people in the music business. Where do you think he got those names? And their secrets?"

"I don't know!" Pac snapped. "Why do you keep asking me these questions?"

"Because, Andy," I said, "I think you know more than you're saying."

"Like—like what?"

"I think you know why Corky wanted to hire me. I think you knew Felix Nolan. I think you had something to do with this whole thing."

"I—I don't know anything," he insisted. "Corky and Walter, they keep everybody in the dark. It's always just the two of them doing—doing things."

"What kind of things?"

"You know, things . . . schemes . . . deals . . ."

I realized I was stalling. I was waiting for him to give himself away, and he was too smart for that.

Then, suddenly, I became aware of it. I sniffed the air, moved further into the room and sniffed again.

There it was. Not as strong this time, but it was there.

That's where I had smelled that cologne. In the restaurant where I'd questioned Andy Pac before.

He was the guy who wore that cologne I'd smelled on the bridge, and in my closet.

Andy Pac *was* the guy.

52

I STEPPED INTO THE ROOM AND CLOSED THE DOOR behind me.

"W-what are you doing?" he asked, nervously.

I'm not a big guy, but men like Andy Pac are intimidated easily. He was not a big man, and very thin—like the man on the bridge that night. I couldn't match the voices because the man on the bridge had been disguising his, but they seemed the same size. And then there was the cologne.

I walked to his desk and placed both my fists on it, then leaned in.

"Andy, what's that cologne you're wearing?"

"My—my cologne?" he asked. "W-why do you want to know that?"

"Because," I said, "I smelled it on the bridge that night when I gave you the case, and I smelled it in my closet when you slammed me in the face with the door."

"I don't know—"

"I smelled it in the restaurant the other day, but it

didn't register then. Maybe you didn't put on as much that day as you usually do." I sniffed the air. "Seems like you took a bath in it this morning. Don't you know a little goes a long way?"

"Look," he said, pushing his chair back, "I don't know —" He started to rise, but I cut him off.

"No, you look!" I snapped. "Sit down!"

He sat and looked around as if hoping to find an escape hatch. He looked longingly at the door, but couldn't get past me to it.

"Don't try telling me you don't know what attaché case I'm talking about, Andy. I found your business card in it."

"What?"

I showed him. It wasn't the same card I had found; it was one I'd just palmed from the top of his desk. But how was he to know?

Interrogation was not my strong suit, but I'd recently had a chance to study Detective Hollinger at work.

I kept my tone even and low.

"I found Felix Nolan's notebook, with all the names in it that you gave him."

"I don't—I don't—" he stammered.

"You don't know what I'm talking about? Well, I think I have enough to go to the police with, Andy. Maybe you'll be able to talk to them."

"You—you haven't gone to the police yet?"

"No, I haven't," I said.

Pac moved faster than I would have thought. He opened the top drawer of his desk and came out with a gun, a .38 revolver.

"You're kidding me," I said, as he pointed it at me.

"I can't let you go to the police," Pac said.

"So what are you going to do, shoot me here in your office?"

"Only if I have to."

I hadn't looked down the barrel of a gun since Afghanistan. There was a cold feeling in the pit of my stomach. I didn't know Andy Pac well enough to think he wouldn't shoot me. Hell, he was so nervous I figured he might shoot me by accident.

"Andy," I said, "let's work this out."

"It sounds like you already worked it out, Auggie," Pac said.

"I figure you've been feeding names to Felix Nolan for him to blackmail. Maybe you've been in for a percentage. Is it worth murder for you to keep that quiet?"

"You've got to shut up now and let me think."

"Andy," I said, "did you kill Nolan?" I figured I had to keep talking until I could think of something.

"Shut up!" he said. He was close to tears. His eyes were watery and darting around behind his thick lenses.

"People know I was coming here, Andy."

"But not the cops," he said. "I guess maybe you shouldn't have told me that, Auggie."

Yeah, well, I was guessing the same thing.

"What about my guitars, Andy?" I asked. "What was the point of breaking into my place and trashing my axes?"

"We—we were just trying to give you something else to think about," he said. "I-I didn't want to do it, but they made me."

"Who made—"

"Damn it, shut up, Auggie!"

At that moment the door opened and Walter Rutlidge walked in. He stopped short when he saw Andy holding a gun on me.

"Andy," he said, "what the hell are you doing with that gun?"

I hoped that Andy would move the gun and point it at Walter. If he did that, maybe I could've made a move, but he disappointed me and kept that gun pointed right at my belly.

"Auggie?" Walter asked. "What's going on?"

"This is your man, Walter," I said. "He was working a blackmail scheme with Felix Nolan. My guess is they fell out over the masters, and Andy killed him."

"What?" Walter looked at Pac. "Andy is this true?"

"Yes," Andy said, then, "no. I don't know."

"What do you mean, you don't know?" Walter asked. "Either you killed Nolan or you didn't."

"I didn't—" Andy said, haltingly. "I didn't kill him. That was them. But I did know him."

"And the blackmail?"

"I—I never blackmailed anyone, Walter. I only gave him information."

"Information that he could use to blackmail people," I pointed out.

"I—I don't know what he did with it."

"Trust me, Andy," I said. "He was blackmailing them all. And if you didn't get a piece of the action, why were you giving him the names and information?"

"Andy," Walter said, "I can't believe this."

"Okay," Pac said, "okay, you both have to be quiet now. I have to think. Close the door, Walter."

"Andy—"

"Close it!"

"You know him better than I do, Walter," I said. "Will he shoot?"

Walter stared at Andy Pac for a few moments, at the

look in his eyes and the shake of his hand. Finally he said, "I'm not sure."

"Well then," I said, "I'd suggest you do what he says. Close the door."

53

WALTER RUTLIDGE RELUCTANTLY CLOSED THE DOOR, then turned to face Andy Pac.

"We have to get out of here before somebody else comes looking for you two," Pac said.

"How are you going to—"

"Shut up!"

I looked at Walter. I'm sure he was as scared as I was, but he looked cool enough.

Pac looked lost. He glanced at his landline, then at his cell phone, which was sitting on the desk next to it. Okay, he wanted to call someone. That meant there was somebody else involved, somebody he thought would be able to tell him what to do, but he didn't want to make that call in front of us.

Finally, he picked up the cell, hit a button with his thumb, then held the phone to his ear.

"Yeah, it's me . . . We've got a problem . . . the PI, Velez, is here . . . Yeah, he knows enough . . . No, no, I got the drop on him, but . . . . Yeah, but, Walter Rutlidge walked in on us . . . Yeah, I'm holding it on both of them . .

. Well, I didn't know what to do . . . What. . . Yeah, I can do that . . . don't talk to me like that!"

But the person on the other end appeared to have hung up already.

"I—I want you both to put your cell phones on the desk."

"What for?" Walter asked.

"Just do it."

Walter hesitated, but I took my phone out and did as I was told.

"Walter," I said.

He frowned, but took out his phone and put it next to mine.

Andy stood up, awkwardly put his jacket on, switching the gun from hand to hand to do it. Then he grabbed his cell phone and put it in his jacket pocket.

"I'm going to put the gun in my pocket with my hand on the trigger and we're going to walk out. If you say anything to anyone, I'll shoot them. Understand?"

"We understand," I said.

Walter nodded.

"Open the door, Walter," Pac said.

"Where are we going?" I asked.

"Shut up!" he snapped, starting to sound like a broken record. He put the gun in his pocket, pointing it at us like he was in a bad movie.

"Very good, Andy," Walter said. "No one will notice us that way."

Pac looked down at himself, then relaxed his hand a bit, so it wasn't so obvious he was holding a gun on us. Walter had been very helpful.

"Open the door, Walter. You're both going to walk ahead of me. If one of you runs, I'll shoot the other one."

That made me wonder about Walter. Maybe he'd figure he could run, and Andy would be too busy shooting *me* to shoot *him*. That thought didn't fill me with confidence.

Walter opened the door and we stepped out into the hall.

"Where are we going, Andy?" I asked.

"Walk to the elevator."

We walked down the hall to the elevator without passing anyone.

"Up or down?" I asked.

"Very funny," Pac said. "Down."

I pressed the down button. I wondered what Pac would do if the doors opened and Corky Barnes was standing there. It didn't happen, though. The doors opened and the car was empty. Wasn't anybody taking a late lunch in this building?

"Inside. Press one."

We did as we were told, and I pressed one.

"Please don't try anything in the lobby," he pleaded. "A lot of innocent people could get hurt."

"Don't worry, Andy," I said. "We're not going to try anything . . . are we, Walter?"

Walter Rutlidge was starting to look nervous. If the doors opened and he bolted, we'd all be in trouble.

"Walter?"

"No," Walter said, "n-no, we won't."

I prepared myself to grab Walter if he panicked and tried to run, but the doors opened and he just stood there.

"Step out."

No one was waiting for the elevator, but there were a few people in the lobby, and I could see a couple out in front, smoking.

"Hello, Mr. Rutlidge," the security guard said as we walked to the front doors.

"Hi, Al," Rutlidge said. I found myself hoping the guard's name wasn't Al, but he didn't seem concerned as we went by.

Outside we went past the smokers, who didn't speak to Pac or Walter.

"Where's your car?" Pac asked me.

"Near the park."

"Walk to it."

"Why take me, Andy?" Walter asked as we started walking.

"I can't leave you behind, Walter," Pac said, "You might call the police."

"What if I gave you my word—"

"Just keep quiet, Walter," Pac said. "No more talking."

Walter fell silent.

When we reached my car Pac said, "Wait."

He was thinking, trying to figure out how we would all get inside.

"All right, open the driver's door. Walter, you get in first and slide over, then you, Auggie. I'll be in the back, and I'll have you both covered."

We did as we were told. He slid into the car behind us. We slammed the doors.

"Now what?" I asked.

"Drive."

"Where to?"

He hesitated, then said, "Germantown."

"What's in Germantown?" Walter asked.

"You'll see when we get there."

. . .

WE WERE HALFWAY to Germantown when I looked in the rearview mirror at Andy Pac. He was biting his lip, fighting back the tears, his watery eyes darting about as he wrestled with his situation.

Abruptly, I pulled the car to the curb and cut the engine.

"What are you doing?" Pac yelled. "I didn't tell you to stop."

"What *are* you doing, Auggie?" Walter asked.

"I'm not going any further," I said.

"Auggie—" Walter said, warningly.

"No," I said, "if he wants to shoot, let him shoot." I turned in my seat, found myself looking down the barrel of the .38. My heart almost stopped, but I kept staring. "Andy, I think you're in over your head and you need help. I'm willing to help you."

"What?" he asked. "Why?"

"Because I don't think you killed Nolan," I said. "But I think you know who did. Or, at least, you know who he was working with. That person probably killed him."

"Y-yeah," Pac said, "probably."

"Then tell me who it is," I said. "I'll take him down. And I'll tell the cops you cooperated."

He bit his lip again, then said, "Will you let me go?"

"I can't do that, Andy," I said, "but it'll help that you cooperated."

"I can't go to jail!" Pac yelled. "I can't!"

"Jesus, Andy," Walter Rutlidge said, "if you're not going to shoot us, why don't you just shoot yourself?"

Pac's eyes started bouncing around in his head, again. I waited for him to squeeze the trigger, wondering if I was wrong about him when suddenly he put the gun under his chin and pulled the trigger.

54

"CHRIST!" WALTER SHOUTED.

The top of Andy Pac's head exploded onto the interior roof of the car. The bullet went right through.

"Why the hell did you tell him to do that?" I demanded, turning around to face front again. I felt sick but held on to the contents of my stomach.

"I didn't think he'd really do it!" Walter shouted back. "Jesus. What about you? Why didn't you just tell him you'd keep him out of jail? Or let him go?"

"I guess I should have," I said.

We sat in silence for a moment and then I heard a sound. It was a few more seconds before I realized it was the sound of Andy's brains dripping from the ceiling of the car. That was it. I opened my door, leaned out and vomited onto the pavement. When I finished barfing, I could hear Walter doing the same on his side. Then we both got out of the car, stepping carefully.

Across the street a jogger was running by, staring at us. I didn't know if she'd heard the shot, but she certainly saw me being sick.

Walter was leaning back against the car on his side, being careful not to look inside. I walked around and leaned next to him. My hands were shaking. I wasn't sure I was done barfing.

"Jesus . . ." Walter said. "That was horrible."

I didn't point out again that it was his idea.

"What are you going to do now?"

"I'm thinking, Walter," I said. "It's not like I deal with situations like this every day." Then something occurred to me. "He was making me drive us to Germantown."

"So?"

"That's where Felix Nolan lived," I said.

"So what are you thinking?"

"That Nolan had a partner, maybe somebody who lived right in his building."

He studied my face for a moment, then said, "You're reaching. You've got no way of knowing that."

"But what if I'm right? What if his partner's in that building, along with the masters?"

"So what do you propose we do? Drive there with a body in the car?"

I turned, looked through the window at Andy Pac's body and almost puked again.

"No," I said, looking away, "I can't do that. But I can't just dump him. I'll have to leave my car here and catch a cab somewhere."

"I can't go with you. I'm simply not that brave. Do you understand?"

"I understand, Walter."

I thought I could use Andy's cell phone to see the number he'd last called, and his gun. But I knew taking each wouldn't be easy. I'd not only have to get in the back seat with him, but I'd have to . . . touch him. And removing both from the scene would get me in trouble with the cops. But if I was going to be facing a murderer, I'd need that gun.

I pushed away from the car and walked around to the driver's side rear door.

"What are you doing?"

"I need his cell phone, and his gun."

"Auggie, I'm not a criminal lawyer I'd advise against taking anything out of the car. It's a crime scene."

"I'll have to take that chance."

"Well . . . try not to get any . . . brains on you."

I opened the door and Walter turned away. I looked up at the ceiling to see if any more pieces of . . . Andy was going to drip, then leaned in carefully. The gun was easy, as it was lying on the floor. Andy's leg had kept anything from getting on it.

The cell would be harder. It was in his right-hand pocket. I had to close the car door, go around and open the other one. After I was sure nothing was dripping, I reached in with my fingertips and plucked the cell phone out of his pocket. Then I backed out so quickly I banged my head.

"Shouldn't you use a handkerchief for that?" Walter asked.

"Why? It's obvious the phone and the gun are Andy's. You're my witness and I'm yours, Walter."

I closed the door, then used my key to lock the car.

"Now what?" Walter asked.

I looked down at Andy's phone. I tried to get a dial tone, but the battery must have been low.

"Get to a phone and call Detective Hollinger. Tell him what happened, where Andy is, and where I've gone. If I'm right about this, I'll be ready to hand everything I know over to him."

"I'll do that. Watch yourself, son."

"I intend to, Walter," I said.

We walked in opposite directions and I took a deep breath, as there was a good chance this was the last clear air I'd get to breathe before the cops tossed me into prison.

55

I FELT BAD ABOUT LEAVING ANDY'S BODY BY THE SIDE OF the street in my car, but he could be picked up later. I walked a few blocks before I was able to flag down a cab, and had him take me to Felix Nolan's building in Germantown.

The cab dropped me off a block away; I walked the rest of the way. I had Andy's gun in the right pocket of my windbreaker, and his cell in my left. I took the phone out and tried looking at the last number called. It came up but didn't mean anything to me.

What was I supposed to do now? Whoever Andy had called was expecting the three of us. Was I right? Were we headed here? Should I go rushing in with the gun in my hand?

I pressed redial. The connection was made, but nobody spoke. I kept quiet and listened.

"Andy?" a voice finally said. A woman. "Are you on the way, man?"

I didn't answer, and she broke the connection. I tried to call the police, but again the power was low. I must have used the last of it to redial. I put the phone in my pocket. Hitting redial had accomplished my goal.

The voice belonged to Nolan's neighbor from across the hall, Melanie.

I ENTERED THE BUILDING, hoping Melanie hadn't been looking out the window as I arrived. I went up the stairs to Nolan's floor, using the stairwell.

I opened the door and peered out. No one by the elevator, no one in the hall. I slipped out, hurried to Melanie's door. I knocked and waited.

"Come on in, Andy," she called out.

I started to open the door, then paused to put the gun in my pocket. It wouldn't surprise her, me walking in first. She wouldn't realize Andy wasn't behind me until I was inside, and closed the door behind me.

I opened the door and entered.

She was standing in the center of the room, dressed similarly to the last time I'd seen her—cutoffs and a T-shirt. Her thumbs were hooked into her pockets. It was a pose that had served her well over the years.

I closed the door.

"Jesus," she said, "he fucked it up, didn't he?"

"He must've been really scared of you, Melanie," I said. "He blew his head off."

"With the gun we gave him," she said, shaking her head. "I knew he'd screw this up, eventually."

"So Nolan's dead, and Andy's dead," I said. "Did they recruit you?"

"Them recruit me?" she repeated. "Ha! Those two were small time before they met me."

"Are you telling me the blackmail was your idea?"

"No, that was them," she said. "Felix met Andy at a club one night. They got drunk and hatched this plan because Andy didn't have the balls to do the actual *deed*, but he had the information."

"How'd you get involved?"

"I told you," she said. "I slept with Felix a few times. He started telling me how he made his money, and I saw a chance to take over."

"So you kept them both in line?"

"Oh yeah," she said, "I kept giving both of them a taste from time to time. Andy, the nerd, he loved it. Couldn't get enough. He'd do anything I told him."

"And when you heard about the recording masters you figured to take them to the big time."

"Can you believe it? Felix was satisfied with what he was pulling in, even splitting it. But a million dollars," she said. "For a really bad Patsy Cline album."

"And Elvis," I said. "Don't forget Elvis."

"I never would!"

"A million dollars," I said, "times two. How did you get Andy to kill Nolan, and meet me on the bridge?"

"Andy kill Nolan?" she asked, laughing. "Don't you think if he'd done that you'd be dead by now?"

"So who killed him? You?"

"He didn't want to do it," she said. "Felix wanted to stay small time. So he had to go."

"And you did it?"

"No," another voice said, "I did."

I looked over at what was probably the doorway to her bedroom. A man was standing there, pointing a gun at me — an automatic. I cursed myself for having put Andy's gun in my pocket.

"Baby, see if he's got Andy's gun on him." To me, he said, "Just keep your hands up, friend."

"Just stand still, dude," she said to me.

"Don't get between me and him," the other man said. "Go around behind him."

She did as he said and reached into both pockets, coming out with the gun and phone.

"Anything else?" the man asked.

"No."

She moved away from me.

"I know you," I said, finally recognizing him. "You were asleep on the sofa last time I was here."

"Some guys gotta sleep," he said, with a shrug, "and some guys gotta die."

56

"Yeah," I went on, "you're the guy she said likes to fuck her in the butt so you can pretend she's a guy."

He frowned and said, "W-wha-a-a-t?"

"Don't listen to him, sugar," Melanie said. "I'd never say nothin' like that about you."

"Yeah, okay," I said, giving the guy a look. "Look, pal—"

"Shut up," he said, then looked at Melanie and asked belligerently. "You sayin' I'm a fag?"

"Jack, would I be fuckin' you if you *was* gay?" she asked. "Come on! This guy's just tryin' to rattle you."

"You've got more problems than being gay, Jack," I said.

"Whataya talkin' about?"

"Aren't you asking yourself where Walter Rutlidge is?"

Jack frowned at me. I could see who the brains of this outfit was. Melanie must have been playing Felix, Jack and Andy.

"The lawyer," I said, to clear it up for him. "He was in the car with me when Andy blew his brains out."

"Yeah," Jack said, "Where *is* the lawyer?"

"He's calling the cops," I said. "In fact, he probably already did it a while ago. They should be here any minute."

"He's bluffin', right?" Jack asked Melanie.

"Probably not," she said. "We better get him out of here and then kill 'im."

Jack raised his gun and sighted down the barrel at me. My stomach clenched.

"I said," Melanie shouted, "get him out of here and *then* kill him! You can't shoot him here."

Jack lowered the gun.

Melanie said, "Wait here. I gotta put somethin' else on and then we'll get out of here." She dropped the gun and cell phone onto the sofas and went into the other room.

"Jack," I said, "you've got more to think about."

"Like what?"

"Felix is dead and Andy is dead."

"That just makes for a two-way split," he said.

"Well, that's good math," I said, "but think about it. Maybe Melanie would prefer a one-way split."

"You sayin she'd try to kill me?" he asked. "She wouldn't do that."

"Why not?"

"She loves me."

"That's why she was trying to get into my pants while you were sleeping on the sofa?"

"She's just a sexual girl," he reasoned. "Sex ain't got nothin' to do with love."

I stared at him. He was wearing a T-shirt and jeans, looked to be about ten years younger than Melanie.

"Jack," I said, "come on. She's been playing you just the way she played Felix and Andy."

"You shut up!"

"What's he sayin'?" Melanie asked, coming back into the room wearing her jeans. She still had on the same tight top.

"He's tryin' ta make me think you'd kill me for all the money."

"Of course he is," she said. "He's trying to save his ass by getting you to turn on me."

She walked to the sofa and picked up the gun.

"Come on," she said, holding it carelessly, "let's go."

"Why don't you put that away before it goes off?" I suggested.

"What, this?" She brandished the gun. "I make you nervous?"

"It might go off," I said, "You wouldn't want that, right? You don't want the neighbors hearing the noise."

"Don't worry," she said. "These guns aren't gonna go off —accidentally. At least, not until we get you someplace safe."

"Someplace safe," I repeated, then more to myself, "someplace more . . . private?"

"Yeah," she said, "more private. Now move."

"No."

"What?"

"I'm not moving," I said, "and you're not going to shoot me here. You can't risk the shot being heard."

"You're right," Melanie said, "but don't make me get a knife from the kitchen, Auggie. Or maybe I'll use a pillow to silence the shot." She looked at Jack. "I saw that on TV."

"Yeah, I saw that, too," he said.

"But then you'd have a body in your apartment," I said. "How would you get rid of it?"

"I'll just have Jack drag you over to Felix's apartment," she said. "It would be a while before they found you there, sugar."

She had all the answers.

"So how do you want to do this?" she asked.

"Like you said," I answered, "let's go."

57

I FELT FAIRLY SURE THE POLICE WOULD ARRIVE BEFORE they could take me out of the building. Of course, that was if Walter had called when he said he would.

They walked me down the stairs to the first floor. They both held their guns down by their sides.

"Where's your car?" she asked, as we got the front.

"I had to leave it," I said. "Andy killed himself in it. Remember?"

She looked at Jack.

"We'll have to use yours," she said.

"It's actin' up."

"We don't have to go far," she told him. "Just East Germantown."

"Okay. It's over here."

I looked around as Jack walked us to his car. No cops. I was starting to think I was seriously fucked, but oddly I wasn't scared. I was just mad. There had to be a way out of this. In Afghanistan, we often got our butts in a sling, but we always found a way out. Why should this be any different?

Jack's car turned out to be a piece of shit Hyundai, a four-door with lots of body rust. Had to be ten or eleven years old.

"Crap," Melanie said, shaking her head.

"Never been in his car before?" I asked.

"Not on a bet."

I looked at Jack. "Why didn't you buy a new one with the blackmail money?"

"Nothing's wrong with this one."

I stared at him.

"Besides," he added, "she wouldn't let me spend any of it."

He unlocked the door and got in on the driver's side.

"You're in the front, Auggie," Melanie said. "I'll be in the back seat with my gun on you."

"Got it."

"If you try anything, I'll shoot you. Understand?"

"I figured that was implied," I said, "but yeah, I understand."

"You're smart," she said, "and cute. We coulda had some fun, sugar."

Jack started the car. It coughed, spit black exhaust, then started.

"Where we goin'?" he asked Melanie.

"Head for East Germantown, the river," she said. "We need a nice quiet spot to dump a body." She put a hand on my shoulder and squeezed. "We'll have some fun now, sugar bear."

58

EAST GERMANTOWN. WE WEREN'T FAR FROM THE storage unit Chummy and I had been in.

"Head right for the river's edge," she said. "We can do it down there."

"Why don't we talk about this?" I asked.

"What's to talk about, Auggie?" she asked. "It's pretty clear you're the good guy and we're the bad guys."

"Why don't you just drop me off and make a run with the money?" I asked. "You have over a million, right?"

"We have the chicken feed we've been taking off people for months," Jack said, "but we don't have our share of the million yet."

Yet?

"Shut up, Jack!" Melanie snapped.

Sullenly, Jack fell silent.

"Besides," Melanie said, "it's not like you'd keep your mouth shut."

"What if I said I would."

She stroked the back of my head with her free hand and said, "I'm afraid I wouldn't believe you, sugar."

I couldn't see any way out. I seriously wished I'd just stuck to my music.

MELANIE DIRECTED Jack to a clearing down by the river. Behind us, in the distance, were a few buildings. Across the river some hills and a building or two.

"Get out," Melanie ordered.

I stepped out of the car to find both Jack and Melanie pointing their guns at me. I was amazingly calm. I didn't think Jack had what it took to murder me. Melanie was another story, but I was pretty sure I was fifty percent safe.

"Down by the water, Auggie," Melanie said, gesturing with her gun.

We walked down to the water's edge, and I turned to face them. The river was on my right—on their left.

"Okay, Jack," she said, "do it."

"Do what?"

"Kill him."

Jack's eyes went wide. He looked at me, then back to her.

"You want me to shoot him?"

"You got a gun, don't you?" she asked. "Shoot him, baby. You're my man, right?"

"Well, yeah . . ."

"Then kill him," she said. "Do it for me."

Jack swallowed, raised his gun and pointed it at me. I could see in his eyes he wasn't going to do it. Finally, his arm dropped as if the gun was too heavy.

"I can't," he said. "I guess I ain't a killer, Melanie."

"Looks like you're going to have to do it yourself, Melanie," I said. I was already fairly sure I was looking at two people who weren't killers. And that meant they hadn't killed Felix Nolan, either.

"Shut up, Auggie," she said. She pointed the gun at me, but quickly lowered it.

"You guys aren't killers," I said. "Just blackmailers."

"Damn it!" Melanie said, obviously disappointed in both of them. "You gotta let us go, sugar."

"I don't know if I can do that," I said, "but first, let me have the guns so that they don't go off by accident."

I stepped toward Jack and he held the gun out to me. At that moment I saw blood suddenly blossom on his chest and he went down backward. It was only then I heard the shot.

"What—" Melanie said.

"Sniper!" I shouted. "Down!"

But she was so shocked she just stood there, staring down at Jack. The only thing for me to do was tackle her to the ground. I grabbed the gun from her hand and shielded her with my body while I looked for the shooter. I was having flashbacks to Afghanistan. Obviously, he'd taken the shot from far off. The revolver in my hand was useless, but I clutched it anyway, just for comfort.

"What's happening?" Melanie gasped.

"Just lie still," I said.

There was no cover near us. I was exposed while I was shielding her, an easy target for someone who had been able to make that first shot, but another shot didn't come

We stayed that way for what seemed like hours, and then I decided the shooter was gone. Maybe he'd meant to take more shots, but in the end, there was only that one, and Jack paid the price.

"Jack—" Melanie said, looking over at her dead boyfriend.

"Let me have your cell phone, Melanie," I said. "It's time to call the cops."

59

I DIDN'T MUSTER OUT OF THE MARINES WITH THE REST of my unit. I still wasn't over Jimmy's death, and how it had occurred, so I re-upped and signed up for sniper training. After I earned the right to be called a Marine Corp Sniper, I spent the rest of my second tour of duty in Afghanistan doing to the enemy what they had done to Jimmy.

It didn't help, but the training stays with you . . .

I SPENT the rest of the day and part of the night in an interview room. Hollinger and his partner, Lewis, took their turns at me. We talked about the Nolan murder case, blackmail, about Andy Pac's death, about Jack and Melanie, and about the shooting by the river. Over and over again, as they tried to catch me in some kind of lie.

My eyes felt gritty and raw; I could smell my sweat as Hollinger came in at one point with two cups of coffee. He sat down across from me and pushed one over to me.

"You're in trouble, Auggie."

"I've been threatened with guns, and shot at," I said. "How does that put me in trouble?"

"You didn't call in the Andy Pac shooting right away," he said. "You left the scene, removed evidence—"

"—and found your blackmailers for you," I added." And when I did, I called you."

"After one of them got killed."

"After," I said, "I was sure they weren't going to kill me."

I sipped my coffee and sat back in my chair.

"The girl corroborates your story," he said. "She also says you saved her life by covering her with your own body. Tell me something, Auggie? Why aren't you dead, too? Why didn't the shooter kill you, and then finish the woman?"

"I don't know."

"Obviously," Hollinger said, "he didn't want to kill you."

"Maybe he had orders, and I wasn't included."

"Orders from who?"

"I don't know."

"You know," he said, "we have the blackmailers, that's true. But we don't have the killer."

"Maybe Pac killed Nolan, and now he's killed himself."

"There's no way we can prove that. Of course, the woman or the dead guy, they could've killed Nolan, either one of them or together."

"Uh-uh," I said. "They didn't have it in them. They couldn't kill me, not even to keep me quiet. I was about to disarm them both when the sniper started shooting."

"Sniper?"

"Well, that's what they were in Afghanistan," I said. "That's how I thought of the situation today."

"And that's why you shielded the woman and left yourself exposed?"

"I guess so," I said. "I guess old instincts die hard."

"Or," he said, "you knew the shooter wouldn't kill you."

"You're going to have to let that go, Hollinger," I said. "If I wanted the shooter to kill them both, why would I get in the way?"

"Good question."

"Look, are you going to charge me with anything?"

"I think maybe," Hollinger said, "it's time for you to tell us the whole story. Everything you've been holding back. And then we'll see about charging you or not."

I took a deep breath and blew it out. He was probably right. The whole thing had gotten out of hand. Three men were dead, Melanie and I had come close. I'd covered for Corky Barnes long enough.

I told him all about the Patsy Cline and Elvis Presley masters.

"A MILLION DOLLARS?" he asked. "For bad recordings?"

"For early recordings of Patsy Cline and Elvis," I corrected.

"So where are they?" he asked. "Who's got them? And who's got the million?"

"I guess that's for you to find out," I said. "I think I'm done with it all."

"Are you sure Jack and Melanie didn't have it?"

"They said they hadn't gotten their share of the million, yet," I said. "That's what they were waiting for."

"From who?"

"From whoever has the masters and the million."

"And you believed them?"

"Yeah, I did."

He thought a moment, then stood up.

"Are you letting me go?"

"Sit tight," he said. "I have to talk to Melanie again. Hopefully, she hasn't lawyered up yet."

"And what about my lawyer?" I asked.

"Rutlidge is outside," he said. "I told him I'd let him talk to you as soon as I was done. I'll send him in."

"Hey, Hollinger."

He stopped at the door. "What?"

"How come you didn't drive to the Nolan address when Walter told you that's where I was going?"

"When did he tell me that?"

"When he called you to tell you where to find Andy's body, and where I went."

He shook his head. "He never called—not *me*, anyway."

"What about nine-one-one?"

"No calls to nine-one-one, Auggie—not from Germantown."

60

I HAD A FEW MINUTES TO THINK THINGS OVER BY THE time Walter Rutlidge entered the room.

"I'm trying to get a criminal lawyer over here for you, Auggie," he said, "but for now you're stuck with me."

"Why don't you sit down, Walter?" I invited. "We need to talk."

"About what?"

"Go on, have a seat."

Walter sat down across from me, where Hollinger had been.

"You look tired," he said.

"I am," I said. "Tired of the whole thing. I've also learned a lot . . . about myself, about being a detective . . . and about you, Walter."

"Me? What have you learned about me?"

"Well," I said, "for one thing, you never called Hollinger to tell him about Andy, or about me going after Jack and Melanie."

"I did—well, I didn't call Hollinger," he said, "but I called nine-one-one."

"But nobody came."

"That's not my faul—"

"There were no nine-one-one calls, Walter."

"What's your point, Auggie?"

"My point is, somebody's been behind the scenes pulling strings all this time," I said. "It could only be one of two people—you or Corky. And I don't think it's been Corky."

Walter laughed and asked, "You think it's me?"

"Yes, Walter, I do."

The lawyer sat back in his chair.

"So now you're the great detective? Making deductions? Figuring things out?"

"Not a great detective, Walter," I said. "Not even a good one. Not yet, anyway. But I'm learning how to connect the dots."

"Then connect them."

"I know why you recommended me to Corky," I said.

"And why was that?"

"Because you didn't think I could do the job," I said. "You've been playing fast-and-loose behind Corky's back. When you heard about the masters, you decided to make a move to get rich."

"A million dollars?" he said, laughing. "You think that's rich?"

"Maybe not for Corky," I said, "but maybe for you, yeah. Corky's the one with all the money, right Walter?"

"So I went after the masters? What about Nolan? And Andy and their friends?"

"I think you stumbled into what Andy and Nolan were doing. You figured out that Andy was supplying info to Nolan, and he and his friends were running a little blackmail ring. And you saw your chance."

"To do what?"

"To make some money, get the masters for yourself, and have it all blamed on Andy and his friends."

"So I killed Felix Nolan?"

"You had him killed," I said, "and Andy met me on the bridge instead of Nolan."

"So if I was working with Andy why did he take me in the car with you?" Walter asked.

"So I wouldn't figure out that you were working together," I said. "Or maybe Andy didn't know about you. Maybe you had somebody else contact Andy."

"Who?"

"The same person you had kill Nolan, the same person who shot at Jack today and Melanie. But not me."

"Why not you?"

"Because I'm your man, Walter," I said. "You didn't want me dead. You probably wanted Corky to fire me, eventually."

Walter suddenly frowned at me and leaned forward.

"Did you make a deal, Auggie? With Hollinger? Is he listening in?"

"No," I said. "I only just thought it through a little while ago."

Walter looked around, not convinced that we weren't being recorded or observed.

"You can't prove any of this," he said, finally. "It's all just conjecture on your part—and you're little more than an amateur detective."

"You might be right about that, Walter," I said. "I don't have evidence to give the police. I think you did it. I think you have the million, and you have the masters."

Walter smiled at me then, a smug smile that even if

Hollinger was listening in, even if he was watching, he wouldn't have seen or heard. But I saw it, and I knew.

"Sorry, Auggie," he said, "but you've got nothing."

"I've got nothing to give the police," I said, "but what about Corky?"

"What?"

"What's Corky going to think when I lay this all out for him?"

"He wouldn't believe you."

"Maybe not," I said, "but he's my client. I'll have to make a full report to him. And I'll put all my conjecture into the report. Then we'll have to wait and see what Corky does."

Walter stared at me, not smiling, anymore. At that moment the door opened and Hollinger walked in. For a minute I thought he had been listening in, and maybe he bought what I was selling.

But no . . .

"Okay, Auggie," he said. "You won't need a criminal lawyer. You can go."

"What about Andy? And his gun?"

"Mr. Rutlidge backs your story," Hollinger said. "And the woman does, also. I'm gonna let you walk. After all, you did find the blackmailers."

"What about the killer?" I asked.

"My partner and I will still be working on that," he said. "Don't worry. We'll find him."

"Am I off the hook?"

"You got yourself off the hook," he said.

I stood up, looked at Walter. "You ready to go? You're my ride."

"I'm ready, Auggie. I'm ready."

. . .

WALTER DROVE me to my place, stopped right outside.

"What are you going to do now, Auggie?"

"Walter, I'm going to take a few days before I give my report to Corky," I said. "But just in case anything happens to me, I'm going to give a copy to a couple of friends of mine."

"Why would anything happen to you, Auggie?"

"I don't know, Walter," I said. "You just never know."

"Maybe," he said, "maybe things will have a way of working themselves out."

"Maybe they will, Walter."

I got out and went upstairs.

61

Three days later . . .

HARLEY WAS SITTING on his porch with a drink and a cigar, just as I'd left him last time I was there.

"Get yerself a beer, kid," he said,

"Thanks." I went inside, retrieved a Dos Equis from his frig.

"Good stuff," I said, sitting down.

"You find out who yer friends are when you're sick."

"You got that right."

"So," he asked, "is the case over?"

"For me, it is," I said. "The cops are still looking for a killer."

"Well, if what you told me on the phone is true," Harley said, "the hitter was a pro, so he's already moved onto his next job. The cops will never find him."

"Not my problem," I said. "It was just my job to get those masters back to Corky."

"And did you do that?"

"Funny thing," I said. "Two days after I had my talk with Walter Rutlidge those masters were delivered to Corky by FedEx."

"You're kiddin'."

I shook my head.

"So it *was* the lawyer," Harley said. "You figured it right. I'm proud of you, kid."

"Even though the killer got away?"

"Like you said, catching the killer was never your job. Your client got his property back. But what about the million?"

"Corky doesn't care," I said. "He was very happy to pay to get the masters back."

"And what about your record deal?"

"Ah," I said, "the carrot."

"Did that sonofabitch go back on his word?"

"Not yet," I said, "but he's probably planning to. He told me he'd call me."

"And did you give him your report?"

"I gave him a report," I said.

"You didn't tell him your thoughts about the lawyer?" Harley asked.

"Would he believe me if I did?" I asked. "They've known each other a long time."

Harley thought about it.

"If you tell him his friend made a fool of him, he'd screw you out of your recording deal."

"No doubt."

"And if you don't tell him, the lawyer will feel indebted to you."

"You think so?"

"Oh yeah."

"You don't think he'll bring his hitter back to take care of me?"

"He had his chance to have you killed, Auggie," Harley said. "I have the feeling the guy likes you. Plus, he's probably got his friend's million, which you let him keep."

"Yeah, I did, didn't I? I'm a helluva guy."

"And you got the girl, didn't you?"

I thought about Allegra, who had spent the night in my bed and was probably still there.

"Well," I said, "I got *a* girl."

"So case closed, huh?" Harley asked.

"Case closed."

"And the masters?" he asked. "Have they been authenticated?"

"Not yet, but whether they are or not doesn't really affect me, does it?"

Harley raised his glass. "Here's to Patsy and Elvis. Maybe where they are now they're performing the Honky Tonk Big Hoss Boogie."

I raised my bottle and drank to that.

COMING SOON

The Last Sweet Song of Hammer Dylan (A Nashville P.I. Series 2) from Robert J. Randisi and Wolfpack Publishing.

BOOKS BY ROBERT J. RANDISI

Miles Jacoby Novels

Eye in the Ring

Beaten to a Pulp

Full Contact

Separate Cases

Hard Look

Stand-Up

In Collaboration with Christine Matthews

Murder Is the Deal of the Day

The Masks of Auntie Laveau

Same Time, Same Murder

ABOUT THE AUTHOR

Randisi was born and raised in Brooklyn, N.Y., and from 1973 through 1981 he was a civilian employee of the New York City Police Department, working out of the 67th Precinct in Brooklyn. After 41 years in N.Y, he now resides in Laughlin, NV, 90 miles South of Las Vegas, on the Colorado River, with his 25-year partner-in-life-and-crime, Marthayn Pelegrimas.

He is the author of the "Miles Jacoby," "Nick Delvecchio," "Joe Keough," and "Dennis McQueen," mystery series, and the co-author of the "Gil & Claire Hunt" series. He has been nominated four times for the Shamus Award from the Private Eye Writers of America, in the Novel and Short Story categories.